FAT CHANCE

First published by BCWryter Publishing

First Edition: October 2015
Printed in the United States of America
ISBN: 9781682730768
Library of Congress Control Number: 2015919026
Cover design: Jan Berger

Printed in the United States of America.

FAT CHANCE

Steven R. Berger

She always called me Steven. Not Steve, Stevie or any other diminutive. She helped raise me when my mother came down with tuberculosis. When I was about 10, she asked, "Steven, what would you like to be when you grow up?"

I answered with what I thought was one of the best and most important things a person can be, "A writer."

"I'm sure you will be, and a very good one at that."

She was my Aunt Serena, and this book is dedicated to her.

Serena (Sylvia) Berger
Aug 12, 1914—November 30, 2014

Chapter 1

That was it. Call up the address card on my Mac. Click delete. Confirm delete. And Jasper Acorn was gone.

My long-time friend had been found dead from a heart attack in his home in Santa Barbara three weeks ago by his partner, Jerry. Since Jasper and I had only recently reunited after several years of just going our own ways, nobody thought to call me about the memorial. By the time I heard about Jasper's death, his ashes had been surreptitiously scattered over the vineyard of his favorite local winery. An apt end to a noble, if gluttonous, life.

Another reunion hadn't worked very well for me either. After hooking up again with my college sweetheart on a wild adventure that took me from Denver to Los Angeles to Seattle and back to Los Angeles, we tried being together at her digs in Seattle. Then at mine in Denver. Then by long distance. Then by frequent emails. And then finally, we admitted to each other—and more importantly, to ourselves—that the problems that plagued our relationship in the past, were alive and thriving today. To add insult to injury, she asserted that, despite being the most liberated straight male she knows, I am still somewhat of a chauvinist. At least this time she tempered her tirade by kindly inserting the word "somewhat" before the pejorative "chauvinist."

I've come a long way baby!

A dear friend was dead and my lady fair left me. I guess if Motley, my large Main Coon cat, had run off with someone else, I would have a perfect country and western song. Fortunately, my faithful feline was comforting me with felicitous figure-eights around my ankles and purring loud enough to drown out Led Zeppelin.

Judy Collins was singing Lennon and McCartney's "In My Life," as I mourned both losses. At least, I consoled myself, Morgan O'Connor, and her Bainbridge Island daughter Chelsea, promised to stay in touch.

Jasper, on the other hand, was irreplaceable.

Click.

Delete.

Confirm.

Gone.

I let the venerated vinyl album end. Returned the arm of the ancient turntable to its stand and turned it off. I needed to bring myself out of my depression. I had an article due on children of Holocaust survivors, and a short list of those survivors to interview before I moved on to talk with their children, and then, where appropriate, their children's children.

I focused my thoughts on the present. Everything was okay. Not great, but okay. There are friends and loved ones. There is money enough for the mortgage, necessities and modest pleasures. The car is paid off. I had a gig, and enough freelance journalist work seemed to find me to keep body and soul going. Spirit was lacking. But spirit and enthusiasm have always returned. They will again, I repeated to myself, as if it were a mantra. *Spirit and enthusiasm will brighten my life again. Spirit and enthusiasm will brighten my life again.*

The silly little mantra helped enough for me to flip open my laptop and review the questions I'd been noodling for three days. The exercise was equal parts preparation and procrastination. It seemed that no matter how many hundreds of pieces I've written, each one begins with the feeling of sheer terror. My late wife Heidi, a graphic designer, confessed the same fears whenever she began a new project, despite more than 20 very successful years in the business.

I was satisfied with the questions. They were a good start. I always like to let people lead the interview wherever they want, making them comfortable and gently bringing them back on track as needed. My approach almost always allowed interviewees to open up and tell me the whole story, instead of what they thought I wanted to hear, or worse, how they wanted readers to perceive them.

It was a short drive from my townhome in Denver's Highlands neighborhood—an area my real estate agent swore would be the next Cherry Creek, for which I am still waiting—to that same, chic, Cherry Creek neighborhood where shops and boutiques complement an upscale mall and enhance property values, even in the worst financial times.

Parking is always a thrill in Cherry Creek. But my parking karma led me to a space four spots down from an agglomeration of stately townhomes which, in my dreams, my humble abode will become someday.

I was thinking about my interview. Aaron Meckler is in his late fifties. According to my editor, he is the son of Isaac Meckler, a Polish immigrant who survived three years in a Nazi concentration camp as a young boy, before being liberated by Allied forces. I was impressed that someone who had been through that kind of hell could come to the United States and raise himself up to a standard that enabled his son to live in one of the finest neighborhoods in Colorado.

My speculation and mental preparation was so focused, that I didn't take note of the police squad car near the building. Or, the two, late-model, unmarked, official vehicles with the telltale blue and red strobe lights tucked back behind their grills.

I approached the address I had confirmed with Meckler yesterday, only to find the front door wide open. I ascended the three slate-clad steps in wonder, and cautiously leaned my body through the doorway, careful to keep my feet firmly rooted outside the polished rosewood threshold.

"May I help you?" a handsome woman in a pantsuit asked.

"I came to see Mr. Meckler, Aaron Meckler," I said. Then quickly added, "I must have the wrong address."

As I started to back down the steps the woman froze me in place. "I'm Detective Sergeant Rawlins," she said, "who might you be?"

I was so taken back by the improbability of the situation that I just blurted out, "My name is Sebastian Wren. I'm a journalist. I have an appointment to interview Mr. Meckler. Is there something wrong here, officer?"

"For whom do you write, Mr. Wren?" she asked as she approached me.

"I'm freelance, ma'am. I do magazine and newspaper articles for a number of publications."

"I seem to remember reading an article in *Eco-Mountain Living* about living in harmony with native wildlife, and the author had a bird's name, would that be you?"

"Yes," I answered, the pleasure of having someone remember a bit of my work lighted up my one-word reply like a Broadway opening. But then the matter at hand brought me down like a bad review in the *New York Times*, "Sergeant, is Mr. Meckler here? Is he all right? Is there something wrong? Please tell me what's going on."

"I'm afraid your interview has been canceled, Mr. Sebastian Wren. Mr. Meckler is dead."

Chapter 2

Before I could ask any of the hundred questions that popped up inside my head, I heard the brittle crackling of dry leaves under the wheels of a late model Volvo. It was making a sharp turn into the townhome's driveway and blocking the garages.

A barefoot woman with flowing auburn hair flew from the driver's side leaving the door wide open. The engine had barely stopped before her feet hit the pavement. She ran up the steps toward me and I nearly lost my balance backing away from the door before she came to an abrupt halt imposed by the immoveable barrier that was Detective Sergeant Rawlins. "Just a minute, ma'am," the sergeant said.

"Get outta my way," the woman demanded, tears running down her face. It seemed obvious to me that this was a close friend or family member. But, the sergeant had to stick to the rules, "Sorry, ma'am. Can't let just anyone in. Who are you?"

"I'm his daughter," the redhead answered through tight lips, both her hands clenched into even tighter fists at her sides, "Let me in. Let me see my father."

"I'm sorry ma'am. Please, try to be calm. Tell me your name," Sergeant Rawlins' voice was firm but comforting.

"Adrianne Stark. I mean, Meckler. I'm divorced," she said, as I let those chauvinist traits assert themselves by taking in how attractive this woman was, despite her agitation and a barely noticeable lack of makeup. I took in the nice fit of her paint-splotched jeans and her pink cotton T-shirt, which was similarly paint-splattered.

"May I see some I.D.?" Rawlins said. It wasn't really a question.

"Oh, uh, damn it. It's in my purse. At home."

Sergeant Rawlins consulted her small note pad, "Your address, Ms. Meckler?"

Meckler gave the officer an address on Santa Fe Drive. The number was far enough north to be out of the industrial section, and placed her abode in the revitalized part of the busy thoroughfare where trendy restaurants, shops and galleries now lived—having been chased out of LoDo, the hip name for Lower Downtown—by sky-rocketing rents.

I made a mental note of the three-digit address, guessing that she lived in a studio/loft, which was confirmed when the sergeant asked if that was home or work? "Both," Meckler nearly spit.

"That checks out," Rawlins said. "I understand you're upset, but you shouldn't be driving without your license."

"I'll remember that the next time someone calls and tells me my father's dead," her jaw was tight as a bear trap.

The sergeant wrote something on her notepad and called inside for another officer to escort Meckler into the home. The petite redhead shook off the officer's offer to hold her forearm and crossed the threshold with determination as the sergeant turned her attention back to me. "Now, Mr. Wren. Though I doubt you have any further business here, we need to ask you a few questions. Would you mind stepping into the living room?"

"Of course," I said, following her into a well-lighted living room with contemporary furniture and a baby grand piano. A granite-clad fireplace was flanked incongruously with very old photos in what appeared to be their original, ornate frames. Most were black and white, a few were sepia-toned, and one was a hand-tinted wedding portrait.

"How do you know Aaron Meckler?" the sergeant asked.

"Actually, I've never met him. I talked to him a couple of days ago to set a time for an interview."

"This is for one of your articles?"

"Yes. It's on children of Holocaust survivors. Aaron's father was in a concentration camp, actually, what the Nazis called a 'transit' camp."

"There's a difference?" she asked.

"Yes, though none were what you would call decent living conditions. There were transit camps, slave-labor camps and concentration camps. Several of the countries occupied by the Nazis, along with those who collaborated with them, had camps that imprisoned anyone deemed undesirable, regardless of religion.

"Yes, I knew about the camps, it was horrible. My skin color would have made me a prime candidate for incarceration," Sergeant Rawlins said.

"You're a cop. I'm sure you've seen the same, or worse. Would you mind telling me what happened here?"

"I'm not supposed to say, but, off the record, Mr. Meckler was found dead this morning by his housekeeper. We think it was a suicide. She found him hanged from a beam in his bedroom on the upper floor."

I instinctively looked up when she said that. The roofs on the plush townhomes were pitched. The ceilings were sure to be vaulted, and some would certainly have structural and decorative beams.

"You didn't send his daughter up there to see her father hanging from the rafters?"

"Of course not. The medical examiner has already come and gone. Our boys took him down and laid him out on his bed for the coroner. He's not pretty, you know, his face is purple and all, but he's not hanging there either. Oh. Ma'am,

I'm so sorry. I didn't hear you come into the room," the sergeant said to Ms. Meckler. She had come down the stairs silently, her bare feet as soft as cat paws on the plush Oriental runner. She stared at the two of us for a moment, then turned abruptly on her heel and headed for the hallway. The next sound we heard was retching from what I, for one, hoped was a powder room.

The sergeant and I silently looked to the area where she had disappeared. We heard a toilet flush, and then a faucet run. Then the redhead reappeared. "I'm sorry," she said, "I've seen cadavers before in anatomy class, but . . ."

"It's okay, honey. This is much different," the sergeant tried to console her. "I know I've never gotten used to it. Would you like to sit? Can we get you some water or something? You should take it easy for a few minutes. I'm sorry, but I need you to answer a few questions."

"Yes, thank you. Water would be nice," Meckler said. Sergeant Rawlins nodded at an officer who disappeared into the kitchen.

"Mr. Wren," the sergeant turned to me, "if you're not in a big hurry, I'd appreciate it if you could stick around and give Ms. Meckler a lift back to her place. Besides not having her license with her, she's in no condition to drive. I'll get her keys and we'll get her car back to her when we're done here."

"Sure," I said. I had mixed feelings about staying. Corpses aren't high on my list of things to be around. On the other hand, I was tantalized by being so close to an official police investigation; not to mention, a damsel in distress. I tried to persuade myself that it was my journalistic responsibility to be there and not just my wanton curiosity.

"If I may," Rawlins said, "Ms. Meckler, this is Sebastian Wren. He writes magazine articles and such. He had an appointment to interview your father here this morning. Do you mind if he stays while we talk, and then gives you a ride home?"

Adrianne Meckler looked like a wet sheet hanging from a hook, and sounded worse, "Yeah. Sure. Whatever."

"Ms. Meckler. Please. Try to focus."

"Uh, okay, what?"

The uniformed officer returned carrying the promised water and set it down on the coffee table with a napkin.

"Ms. Meckler. Adrianne. Please drink some water," Rawlins instructed. Meckler took a humming bird-sized sip. "Take another. Make it a big drink this time." Sheepishly Meckler complied. "Any better?"

"Yeah, I guess so," she replied, her voice a few decibels stronger for the hydration.

"Just so I'm sure," Rawlins pressed on, "It's okay with you if Mr. Wren stays for your interview?"

Meckler looked at me as if for the first time. Her shading and features coming back by micro hues, which I attributed to the water and just a smidgen of beginning to get a grip on her situation. "I'm sorry," she said, "Who are you?"

Rawlins looked my way. "My name's Sebastian Wren. I'm a freelance writer. I had an appointment to interview your father this morning. It was for an article I'm doing on the children and grandchildren of Holocaust Survivors. I'm very sorry for your loss."

"You know . . . I mean, you knew my father?"

"No. We spoke on the phone a few days ago. I was looking forward to meeting him. He sounded very interesting."

"He was. He had been a lawyer and judge."

"Can you tell me more about him?" Rawlins jumped into the conversation exactly where she wanted to.

"He was a very kind and generous man . . ." she began.

"Did you two get along?" Rawlins pressed, wanting to cut to the chase instead of wading through all the platitudes and endearing tripe loved ones feel they need to display at the death of a relative.

Adrianne stiffened at the implied accusation. Color raged back to her cheeks. She leaned forward a few inches and was about to speak when she bridled herself, relaxed back and, in a voice as flat as day-old beer, said, "You're right, of course. We didn't always get along. I had a bad marriage he never approved of. But that was past, though I only changed my name back to Meckler last year when the divorce was finalized.

"My Dad helped me through that difficult time, as well as all those mole hills that seemed like insurmountable mountains when I was growing up. He supported, protected and raised me as best he could through the divorce and death of my mother when I was 14, and then two more failed marriages. He was a good man. And, for the last year-and-a-half, my champion and best friend."

She broke down sobbing, and I found myself utterly charmed by her articulate and brave confession. Just on reflex, I went to her side, put my arm over her shoulder and pulled the napkin from under her water glass for her to use as a tissue.

"What else do you want to know?" the strength of her monologue from a moment ago was already waning.

"I'm very sorry I put you through that," Rawlins said with true sincerity. "But we need to find out as much as we can about your father as quickly as possible, and that means finding out about you and anyone else he knew. Do you have any brothers or sisters?"

"No. You'll want to know about Dad's ex-wives. Both got good settlements and, as far as I know, have no ax to grind. As far as my father's associates and colleagues, you can check with the Denver courts, also with the federal prison system."

"Courts and prisons?" Rawlins seemed to grab the question right out of my head.

"I told you, my father was a lawyer and a judge."

"Yes," Rawlins urged her.

Adrianne looked down at her paint-speckled bare feet. "About eight years ago, a young man was found guilty in his court of breaking into the fast food restaurant where he worked. The crucial piece of evidence was an eye witness who said he saw the man leaving the store in the wee hours. The guy had been convicted before on marijuana charges and, when he was just 18, stealing a car and joy riding. Since the B-and-E was his third strike, Dad had no choice but to sentence him to the max, which in Colorado is nine years. And today, the marijuana arrest wouldn't even have made it to court. Anyway, several months later, another man was caught in the act, robbing the same fast food joint. He confessed to the earlier robbery as well. Before the guy who Father sentenced could even file his appeal, he was murdered in prison.

"My father was devastated. He fell into a funk and started to agonize over every decision he had to make from the bench. He felt betrayed by the system. So he retired from the judiciary and began mentoring inmates at the Englewood prison. He wanted to get prisons to help inmates get rehabilitated, not just punished. His depression got better. He felt he was really helping guys, and women in another facility, to improve their educational, social and job skills, and to get ready to reenter society. He was even feeling happy most of the time.

"Of course, his decision to leave the bench affected his income. But he was pretty well off. However, the combination of working with criminals, leaving a prestigious position, and helping me after my divorce, caused his last wife to leave him. He really didn't seem to mind, though. I think he finally found a cause he could believe in, and a way to make a difference."

"Thank you for being so forthcoming and open about you

and your dad, and about his past," Rawlins said, as I tried to take it all in without appearing to be a voyeur.

"There's no use trying to hide anything. That only works in books, movies and on TV. You'd find out all that stuff anyway. Do you think maybe it might not have been suicide?" Adrianne seemed to want to feel better about her father's happiness.

"We can't say at this time, Ms. Meckler. But my own opinion, off the books, of course ..." the detective shot a look at me, " ... is that this was suicide. There's no sign of a break-in or struggle. You've told me enough to convince me that not everything in your father's life was going well. I know it's hard to think he was that desperate, but honey, I've investigated dozens of cases where close relatives and friends, even spouses, didn't see it coming. For what it's worth, I'm sure he took great pleasure in seeing your comeback from what sounds like a pretty bad situation."

Adrianne looked down at her speckled feet again, then tilted her head back to shroud her tears, and whispered, "Thank you."

Chapter 3

We left Aaron Meckler's toney townhome as Detective Sergeant Rawlins had requested. I was hoping the ride to Adrianne Meckler's loft and studio would reveal more about her and her father, as much out of curiosity as compassion. Besides, Adrianne Meckler was on my list of people to interview for my article and she would be more vulnerable and approachable now, I was almost ashamed to admit. But, if I was cautious, this would give me some real insight into the child of a child of a Holocaust survivor, my journalistic instincts told me.

We walked past a huge blue spruce tree and several deciduous trees that had given up their annual leafy ransom to the season. Although it was fall and there was a chill in the air, the bright Colorado sunshine made it feel warmer than it was.

Adrianne's eyes were still red and a bit swollen. Her cheeks seemed more putty. But she still stood tall, given her less-than-average height, and the fact that she was barefoot, despite the chill.

"Thanks for offering me a lift," she said in a flat, lifeless voice.

"Glad to help."

She was very quiet for a minute or two as we drove west from Cherry Creek. Then she turned to me and said softly, "He didn't commit suicide."

Of course not, I thought. Nobody's loved ones ever committed suicide. What was so bad about suicide? Some people are in just so much pain or anguish, that death is a relief. Of course it's really hard on the ones left behind. All those questions. Could I have helped? Why didn't he say something? Didn't he know he was loved? But we really don't know for sure what's hurting someone so bad they just want out, no matter how much we love them.

In answer to my silence she continued redundantly, or forgetting I had been in the room with her and Rawlins. "We weren't always close. But I suppose that's an old story. Most families start together, drift apart, then assume some kind of relationship. But we really got close after my divorce."

I just nodded, wanting her to go on.

"Dad didn't approve of Michael. First, of course, was because Michael wasn't Jewish. But it was more. Dad saw something in him I refused to see. Michael had a very subtle and sinister gift for manipulation. He made others feel that what they were doing was their own idea, not his. He scammed people, with me being the biggest fool of all. First he was buying me records and videos I really liked, so, of course I said 'we should mix all our music and videos together.' Then he insisted we live off what he was earning, even giving me money to go shopping. So, again, I suggested, 'why don't we just have one joint bank account, because we love and trust each other.' But all of that was just window dressing. He really wasn't committed to me. He couldn't open up and share. So our so-called relationship went only so far, because my father wouldn't give in to Michael's scheme to start an internet business—no inventory or assets, just a generous investment from my Dad to create the next Google, Facebook or Twitter. I pleaded with my father to help us. But he insisted we make our own way, the way he and his father did. He said I would never want, and that I was always welcome in his home, but told me his money would go to his grandchildren for their education. He always said that an education is the only thing a *goniff*, or a tyrant or a rascal couldn't take away from you. And with an education, you could always make a new start.

"I'm sorry," she said, "*goniff* is the Yiddish word for a thief, a crook, a scoundrel."

"Thanks, I know. I'm a Hungarian Jew on my father's side," I told her. That got her attention.

"With a name like Wren?"

I liked that she was curious, that maybe she was coming out of her depression. I hoped it would last. I knew it wouldn't.

"Somewhere between Budapest and New York," I pronounced it *Budapescht*, as a good Hungarian would, "some overworked immigration official, or family member, changed or truncated it. My family came over before the war and no one seems to know what happened. I had a great uncle who was a Renkoski, but that's more Russian or Ukrainian or something."

"Maybe your family came to Hungary from there?"

"Certainly a possibility."

"Your mother? Was she Hungarian?"

"No. She's a German *shiksa*," Meckler smiled at my use of Yiddish. "You might say her parents were among the Righteous. Her mother was Lutheran and her father Catholic. He taught at the University. He couldn't abide the persecution of his Jewish and Gentile colleagues. I'm told they hid a few Jews for several days, until the underground could smuggle them out of the country. But a store clerk got suspicious when the man who would become my grandfather bought a suit that wasn't his size. A neighbor mentioned that the clerk was asking questions. They told their underground connections about it, and the next thing they knew, they were all on a train to Marseille, and then on a ship to the US."

"That's like so many stories I heard growing up," she said. "How did your mother and father meet? Was it on the ship? Or through some military deployment?"

"Nothing so dramatic. They met taking English classes at East High night school here in Denver before the US got into the war. Then, of course, the old man got drafted."

"And your wife? Is she Jewish, or part Jewish?"

"I was never completely sure what she was. When we met, she was a recovering Catholic. She studied Buddhism and got into Judaism, along with other philosophies. I don't think she wanted to be nailed down—no pun intended. She just wanted to live the best life she could."

"Past tense?"

"She died several years ago."

"I'm sorry," melancholy shrouding her voice again. "What happened, if you don't mind?"

"It's okay. Leukemia. Her name was Heidi," I said, hoping to mask my sadness.

"A good German name."

"A good movie name," I replied as we drove along Speer Boulevard toward the Santa Fe art district.

"So, which was he?" I asked.

"Uh. Which was who what?"

"Michael. A *goniff*, a tyrant or a rascal?"

"I guess a *goniff*, mostly, like Bernie Madoff. Anyway, after I woke up one morning with an empty bed and an empty bank account, Dad did what he promised. He took me back into his home. Unconditionally. No reprimand. No lecture. No 'I told you so.' He just loved me." A thin veil of tears came to her eyes like a backed up sink at Lourdes.

"He's … I mean, he was, a lawyer. And, for a few years, a judge. He was teaching at Metro and mentoring inmates. He had well-connected friends all over town. He made a few calls and sent me out to meet and talk to people. Three degrees of separation later, a decorator hired me as an apprentice, staging model homes with just the right amount of furniture, just the right color palette, just the right feeling to entice buyers to sign the contract; even baking cookies in show homes for that olfactory seduction sensation. We branched out to do the same thing for real estate listings and really grew the business. I became a full partner. By then I had moved from Dad's townhome in Cherry Creek to a duplex in Highlands Ranch.

"But my passion is painting. Fine art. And the suburbs were sucking the life out of me. So, with my partner's blessing, I sold my share of the business to another up-and-comer. Got a second on the duplex, rented out both sides, and bought my place on Santa Fe for cheap. The rents from the duplex, and the sale of a few pieces each month, takes care of me, the studio and the gallery."

"Pretty shrewd. So, that covers everything?" I asked.

"Now you're acting like a cop. Or a goddamn reporter," she teased.

"Journalist."

"Whatever."

"Sorry."

"Dad was so proud. And yes, he helped me with some money when I needed. More importantly, he supported every decision I made after Michael. That's why I know it wasn't suicide."

"I don't understand?"

"You know about First Fridays?

"Yep. All the galleries on Santa Fe are open late. Put out wine and munchies, and hope they'll sell art."

"It's really very successful. Even if you don't sell something that night, there's almost always a return buyer or a commission that comes directly from First Fridays. I've gotten a number of good hits with work I've shown in other galleries."

"The next First Friday is about a week away."

"Exactly. It will be the first one where I'll be doing a one-woman show in my own gallery, downstairs from my studio and loft."

"And your dad wouldn't miss it for the world."

"Not just that. I own the building. But he's a partner in the gallery. I mean, *was* a partner in the gallery."

Chapter 4

Adrianne's supposition was very persuasive, or maybe I just wanted it to be, for her sake. I was beginning to lose my objectivity. If I wasn't careful, I would screw this up and have to remove her from my interview list. But there was still time to save myself. I was about to suggest that I drop her at her place when my cell phone rang.

Hearing the ring, she turned to me, *"Kind of Blue?"* she asked with a renewed look of calm and grace.

"Actually, *Freddie the Freeloader*, but it's off the Miles Davis *Kind of Blue* album."

I clicked the button on the steering wheel and answered, "Sebastian Wren."

"Wren," a slightly familiar, but not immediately recognizable female said, "this is Detective Sergeant Rawlins."

"Yes, detective. How may I help you?"

"Are you still with Meckler?"

"Yes. You want to talk to her?"

Of course she did, so I pulled my iPhone from my pocket and handed it to Adrianne. As soon as she answered I switched off the bluetooth.

A few moments later, Adrianne handed me the phone, "She wants a word with you."

"Hello detective."

"Are you on speaker?"

"No."

"Good. Can you keep an eye on Meckler for a bit longer? I just asked her if she'd seen a note of any kind in her father's bedroom or around the house. She hadn't. And since she wasn't out of my or another officer's sight since she arrived, we're pretty sure she didn't nick it, if there was one. Anyway, we couldn't find one. And that adds another dimension to this. A man like Meckler would certainly leave a note. Anyway, it would certainly help if we knew that his daughter was with someone."

"Will you be looking for some kind of evidence somewhere else?" I asked pointedly.

She paused just long enough for me to doubt her next statement, "You mean her place? We're sure it won't come to that Mr. Wren. But just the same, perhaps you should take her somewhere for coffee or something? You know, so she doesn't have to be alone just yet."

"Of course," slipped out of my mouth in a sardonic tone before I could check it. I quickly added, "Glad to help. You can reach either of us on my phone for now."

"Thank you," she said, unfazed by my innuendo. "Would you mind calling me after you drop her at her place. We'd like to know where she is to, ah, make sure she's safe."

Yeah, sure, I thought, disliking myself for providing the police a window of opportunity to search her place without her knowledge. I wondered if they would bother with a warrant.

Hanging up, and slipping the phone back into my pocket, I asked Adrianne, "Would you rather get some coffee? A drink? Maybe a bite to eat? Instead of going right back to your place and being alone?"

"Not somewhere public, no. Besides, no shoes, no service," she wiggled her paint-spattered toes. "Do you have anything at your place? I mean a real drink?"

"I've got some micro-brews, a few bottles of wine, 18-

year-old Glenlivet, tequila, and . . ."

"Good, your place it is," she said without a hint of which libation caught her attention.

The ride to my place was quiet. She seemed lost in her own thoughts while I wondered simultaneously about what I was going to do for my article. How long I should babysit this woman? How attractive I found her, and how vulnerable she must be. I wondered if Aaron Meckler had committed suicide? Or if, as Rawlins' recent call had opened the door a crack; had he been murdered? And that made me wonder if Adrianne's ex, Michael Stark might somehow be involved? Doubtful: I read too many mystery novels. He was a con man, not a murderer, at least not that anyone knew of . . . yet.

"Can I turn that up?" Adrianne asked as the radio played the first few bars of Mark Knopfler's "Border Reiver."

"Sure."

She reached over and gave the knob a small twist. The volume stayed up as the free-form college station segued into a very mellow set.

"Highlands," Adrianne said as I pulled my car into the garage behind my townhome. "Very nice. It's going to be the next Cherry Creek."

"You've been talking to my realtor."

"No, it used to be my job. Well, job-related. Anyway, with the economy recovering slowly, it's going to take a while. And it will never actually be Cherry Creek. But it's an up-and-coming neighborhood. Besides, home values only mean something if you're buying, selling or paying taxes. This is a nice area, you should just enjoy it."

"I do," I said, getting out of the car. I didn't even try to get around to her side while we were in the garage, it would have been futile. "One of my best friends and his wife live a few doors down. There's shops, restaurants, even a funky little place for coffee and live music."

"Sounds nice. Maybe later. What this girl needs right now is some of that single-malt Scotch," she resolved the mystery of what to drink as we entered the kitchen from the garage. "Nice place," she said a little too fast for veracity—especially considering her former profession. "Great cabinets, I like the glass doors, oh, there's the liquor, do you mind?"

She didn't wait for my answer. The Glenlivet bottle in her hand, she opened another cabinet with table glasses before I could get to where I the good drinking glasses. She pulled out two juice glasses and set them on the counter.

"Hang on a sec," I said, wondering at her changed, anxious state. I put my keys down on the counter nearest the garage door, stepped in front of her and opened the cabinet with the good glassware. "Here," I handed her a small snifter, "this'll be better."

She poured herself a double and asked if I wanted any. "Maybe later," I said. She didn't down the drink like rail shot whiskey, but she didn't nurse the venerated Scotch the way I like to.

"Do you mind if I have another?" she said, the bottle already resting against the side of the snifter as she looked at me through the eyes of a scolded puppy.

"Go for it," I said, realizing she was in a lot of pain, and putting aside any concerns I would normally have about the cost of the Scotch.

"You wouldn't happen to have any Prozac?" she asked, as she poured herself another double.

"Really, with Scotch?" I was beginning to wonder about this lady.

"You're right," she said "thank you. It's just, fuck, it's so overwhelming."

"Sorry," I said, realizing that all I had was aspirin, Sudafed and—now legal—primo weed. But I wasn't about to go down that road.

She looked disappointed. Then, as if she had gotten a

mental text message, her voice turned to smoke as she said, "Can you turn on some music? That station you had on in the car was nice."

I walked through the dining area to the living room, pushed the power button on the entertainment center and selected the station. Keb' Mo' chimed in with "Dangerous Mood."

Adrianne followed me into the living room and sat down on a burgundy velvet couch. Almost anyone who's new to a home looks around, taking in pictures, art, decor, book bindings and memorabilia, "personality portals," as my Psych 101 professor would say. But Adrianne ignored all that, which I found unusual for someone in the arts, much less the home-decorating business. She looked up at me with those puppy-dog eyes and said, "Why don't you sit down?"

It didn't feel right. But again, I tossed that off to the trauma she'd been through. So I sat down on the couch, a proper distance from her.

Her second drink was more than half gone. She set it down on the glass and copper coffee table. She scooched over and reached her hand up to my cheek, turning my face toward hers. "You know what I really want right now?" I was guessing it wasn't a sandwich and a soda. My mind reeled. She was attractive. It had been a while since I had been with a woman. She was attractive. We had just met, we barely knew each other. She was very attractive. "I want you to fuck me senseless."

I have to admit the thought of making love to her had more than just crossed my mind. But the boldness and coldness of her demand was not music to my ears.

"Sorry, what . . ." I stammered, pulling back, but staying on the couch.

"I really need to get laid. I just want to fuck my brains out," she said, and shook her head from side to side, her long red hair flailing from shoulder to shoulder.

I pulled back farther. "Adrianne. Don't get me wrong. You're a very attractive woman, but you're upset. It's been a long, hard day. I don't think this is really what you want. I'm sure it's not what you need."

She reached out for her glass, tossed back her drink and said, "Where the hell is Clive when you need him." Her face was red with—I'm not sure what—rage? Embarrassment? Flush from the booze? She got up off the couch and started for the liquor cabinet. I knew I had to stop her. Her behavior seemed to be beyond grief, verging on self-destruction. Before she could reach the bottle, the basics of an article I wrote some years ago popped into my head. It was the Prozac and the bold declaration of wanting to bed a complete stranger on a moment's notice, that drew the facts together. But I'm not a psychiatrist, and I didn't want to leap to any conclusions.

Confrontation was out of the question. Intercept and divert were my only options.

"Adrianne, please," I said as I got between her and the booze and put my hands on her shoulders. She pushed her full weight into me. "Please, try to calm down for a moment. You're a wonderful and charming woman who's been through more than anyone should ever have to endure . . ."

She stopped pushing. Stood still as a statue and stared right through me.

"Adrianne, I think I can help, if you'll let me. My friend down the way may have some Prozac or something. I know I said it doesn't go well with alcohol, but I think we should make an exception. Will that be all right with you?"

She continued to just stare at me. I gently turned her back toward the sofa. She didn't resist. As we walked the few steps to the couch I pulled my phone from my pocket and called my neighbor.

"Charles Love," came the identifying answer.

"Charles, it's Sebastian. You home?"

"Down at the precinct," he said. He did IT for the Denver Police Department, among other high-tech gigs.

"Oh," I said, unable to hide my disappointment.

"What's wrong, bro?"

"I've got a situation. I have a lady here that's very upset. She just found out her father died. I was hoping to score her a Prozac or something to help calm her down."

"No Prozac in the house, but Terri might have some Valium left over from when her mom passed. Want me to call her?"

"Yeah, that would be great, tell her it's urgent," I said as Adrianne and I sat back down on the couch.

I held Adrianne's hands in mine and said, "We should have something for you in a few minutes. Is there anything else I can do for you? Do you want to talk about your dad, or anything?" I knew better than to broach the subject of my diagnostic suspicions, which could do much more harm than good, whether I was right or wrong.

"Oh yeah," she said softly, "my Dad. He's dead. He's been murdered." She started to cry and pressed her face into my shoulder. I just held her in silence as the radio offered up Pearl Jam's *Just Breathe*.

It seemed like an hour had passed, but Eddie Vedder was still singing when there was a light knock on the door. I got up gently. Adrianne's face fell into her hands. I opened the door to Terri Love who offered me a prescription bottle saying, "There's six two-milligram tabs. Two tablets should help. Let me know if there's anything else I can do." No questions, no digging for salacious gossip. Just straightforward help and love.

"Thanks," I said as I took the bottle and gave her a kiss.

Chapter 5

I had the morning paper laid out on the table and sipped my coffee as I tried to read the parts not covered by my cat. There were several more cups worth in the carafe. Hot, waiting for my uninvited houseguest. I had heard the shower in the guest bath about ten minutes earlier, ending my quandary about whether to have breakfast on my own, or to be polite and wait for Adrianne.

"Hope I didn't wake you," I lied, as she came into the room, barefoot, hair wrapped in a towel, a cinnamon-colored V-neck T-shirt and her Pollockesque jeans.

"Not sure if it was the coffee grinder, the aroma or just the right time but, may I . . . ?" her hand going for the cup I left on the counter. "Who's your friend?" she asked as she poured.

"This is Motley," I said, as he lifted his furry girth from the paper, jumped to the floor and danced around Adrianne's ankles. "I need to eat soon, can I make you some breakfast?"

"Breakfast too? I was impressed with the new toothbrush and other female-specific accouterments."

"The toothbrush is compliments of my dentist. The lady's necessities were a strong suggestion from a female college classmate years ago."

"Tell her thank you for the clean T-shirt and panties."

"Those were my late wife's."

"Oh, I'm sorry."

"Don't be, she'd be glad to know they went to a good cause. I've got some green chili and black beans mixed with chopped chorizo in the fridge. If you like Mexican, I can have *huevos ranchos* ready in ten minutes."

"Sold. Can I help?"

"Grate some of that Tillamook cheddar, I'll heat the tortillas, fry the eggs and nuke the rest."

"You don't nuke the tortillas?"

"Nope, makes 'em tough. Just throw them right on a gas burner, flip once then pile on the goodies."

She must have been as hungry as me. Barely a word was said from the time the concoction hit the table until we were mopping up our plates with a final tortilla.

"Wow, tampons in the guest bath, you cook, and you wouldn't let me take advantage of you last night. Are you sure you aren't gay?"

"Reasonably certain. Would you like references?" Adrianne smiled. "But since you brought it up . . . "I could see her stiffen at the thought of what I was going to ask next. I decided to just crack the door a little wider and let her open it as much as she wanted, or needed. "Are you feeling okay this morning? Can I get you anything besides underwear and *huevos*? There's more Valium if you need it, but I wouldn't recommend the Scotch."

She smiled in relief, "Mmm, the Scotch was good, but I'll pass. Pills and potions won't bring back my Dad. And, I still have a show to pull together for next Friday." Her shoulders drooped suddenly and in a near whisper she said. "Oh shit. And now I have a memorial to plan too. Oh Sebastian. I guess I should cancel the show. I don't think I can handle it all," tears came in a torrent.

I moved over to the chair next to hers and leaned into a hug. I held her while she sobbed and then surprised myself by saying, "I think you should go through with it. I'll help.

Really, it'll be the best thing. I went through this when Heidi passed. Getting back into the game will help you move on, and it will be an affirmation of what Aaron wanted for you."

"I guess that's what Dad would want. At least that's what everyone always says. But I really believe it. I have to believe it. Did you really mean it? Will you stick around and help? At least for the memorial?"

"Maybe longer. I've always wanted to know how galleries put on a show."

"Be careful what you wish for," she pulled the sides of her mouth back into an imitation smile, tears beginning to dry up.

***

We arrived at her studio around 10:30. "Would you like to come in?" she asked.

"Sure," I had a burning curiosity to see her digs. To peruse her bookshelf, peek at her paintings, nose about where I could. She was a mystery I wanted to unravel like a Dali canvas. Granddaughter of a Holocaust survivor, daughter of a distinguished attorney who may have taken his own life, or been murdered. Divorcée, artist and subject to some very erratic behavior—but that certainly could have been the strain of her father's death.

Santa Fe is a one-way street in her neighborhood. So we had to pass her place, turn right onto a cross street and then turn right again into the alley behind the building. She pointed out the front of the building as we went by. It had a very new-looking slate stone exterior, with large windows and a simple but elegant sign that said AM Art Gallery.

"AM. Adrianne Meckler or Aaron Meckler?" I asked.

"Yes." she answered.

I pulled into a parking space next to the Volvo the police brought back yesterday. And then probably searched the premises. The back of the building was solid looking but could have used a plaster job to repair what had weathered poorly and was blistered and peeling badly. Or, better yet, a sandblasting to just take everything back down to the original brick where a competent contractor would repoint the mortar.

"I wonder where the cops left the keys to your car? I wouldn't leave them in a wheel well or under a floor mat in this neighborhood."

"The neighborhood's not that bad. We all watch out for each other. But I did ask Sergeant Rawlins to have an officer toss them onto the balcony."

I looked up to see where new work on the second level had transformed an old fire escape into a lovely balcony with wrought iron rails that were adorned with intertwined iron vines and grape leaves, affording anyone on the balcony, or in the room beyond, a modicum of privacy. Planters and pots attested to what must have been a thriving flower and herb garden during warmer months. There were French doors that must lead to some part of Adrianne's living quarters.

"Beautiful work," I said.

"One of my neighbors does welding and works on Harleys. I traded him portraits of his kids for the balcony."

"So, you do portrait painting?" I asked as we entered the building through half of a double-door entry secured by a keypad lock.

"Generally no. I used to do that stuff in art school. You've got to learn the disciplines before you break the rules."

"I'll try to remember that."

"Probably no different in writing. I'm sure you tried your hand at fiction, fantasy or poetry before going for journalism."

"Yeah, but you really don't want to see that stuff."

"Go back and look at it sometime. If you still have it. It

probably isn't half as bad as you remember."

"Thanks for the generous vote of confidence," I said as Adrianne entered the gallery.

"What the hell?"

"What? What's wrong?" I pushed past her frozen body and saw what appeared to be several huge walls in a pile. They were predominantly white with splotches of paint on them. I wasn't sure what I was looking at. Could this be some kind of art she did? Perhaps it was some kind of installation? But then the answer came to me in vivid black and red. Her studio had been vandalized.

Still hanging by aircraft cables from the black, structural-steel ceiling, were several more of the white walls. It then became obvious to me that these were merely the back drops where Adrianne would hang her art. And these, along with the ones that had been savagely cut down, were desecrated with swastikas, slashing brush strokes and one crude hammer and sickle. Some also shrieked epithets such as "lesbian liberal," "Jew bitch," "kike cunt" and "commie whore."

I turned back to Adrianne and took her in my arms for the second time since breakfast. She was sobbing again. I wasn't sure if it was for her art, her gallery or her father; probably all three. It didn't matter, she was more than entitled.

It took several minutes for her to regain her composure. All that time I was thinking we need to call the police. Sergeant Rawlins' cell number was on my phone, but I made no move to get it. A few more minutes isn't going to make any difference, I told myself. The important thing is to give this woman the support she deserves.

Finally Adrianne pulled herself together, "I seem to be doing a lot of that lately."

"Don't give it another thought. I'm calling Sergeant Rawlins."

***

Three police officers were at the AM Art Gallery within minutes; the Sergeant arriving seconds later. They probably came from the downtown precinct just blocks away. We met them in the back of the gallery near the large doors where there were restrooms and a small office that apparently had been overlooked by the vandals.

"What happened here?" the sergeant asked as she walked gingerly around the studio trying to figure out who, what, when and how? She already knew where.

When she came to the front door she opened it with ease, despite the deadbolt above the door handle. She turned to examine the door frame and said, "Lookie here."

Adrianne and I, along with two officers, danced our way around the rubble to see what had caught her attention. "Looks like someone took a wood chisel and hammer to the door frame," Rawlins said. "They just chiseled out the bolt holder. Don't you have an alarm in there?" she pointed back into the gallery.

"It hasn't been installed yet," Adrianne answered sheepishly. "That's why nothing was hanging. It's all upstairs," she pointed up a long, straight stairway along one wall that led to what looked like a metal fire door.

"You two secure the scene," she said to the officers. "I want one of you to take pictures of all this and the other to start canvassing the neighbors. Miller should stay in the back for now, check the office and the alley. I'm going upstairs, if that's all right with you, Ms. Meckler?" She was content to get her reply on the run as she started up the stairs.

Adrianne acknowledged her approval by following Rawlins, with me right on their heels.

The landing at the top was larger than it appeared from below. The door was indeed clad in steel, as was the wall fronting the landing, probably for fire protection. Like the front door, this one had a deadbolt. However, both the deadbolt and the area surrounding it on the door, and the steel-clad wall, looked like they had been attacked with an axe. The scars, scratches and pock marks sparkled against the dull gray door and oxidized brass like shimmering rivulets of silver and gold.

But the door had won. It had not been breached.

"You have the key?" Rawlins asked Adrianne.

"Sure. It's on the ring with my car keys . . . and they're on the balcony outside my bedroom."

"If you knew it was locked, why did you ask us to toss your keys onto the balcony?" Rawlins asked.

"I figured I'd just use the one I leave with my neighbor," Adrianne answered. "Sebastian, can I use your phone?" I handed her my cell and she punched in some numbers. "Horse. Adrianne. I'm locked out of my apartment. Can you bring my spare key to the front of the gallery? Right away. Great. I'll meet you there."

"Horse? I'm coming with you," Rawlins said as Adrianne handed me the phone.

"Ahhh, come on. Do you have to?"

"He may be implicated."

"He has a key. The front door and the key to the apartment are the same. He wouldn't need to break in. He's a decent guy, but . . ."

"But he's got a record," Rawlins projected suspiciously.

"Just an old bust from when pot was illegal. He's got a wife and a baby. A good business. Can't you just leave him out of it?"

"If you'll ask him where he was and what he knows about last night, I'll just listen. We can always find him later, right?"

"Thanks."

The ladies got to the foot of the stairs and swung open the

front door. The inspiration for the appellation was immediately apparent. The doorway was eclipsed with the presence of one man—Horse. He had the obvious appearance of a biker: long beard, leather vest, heavy boots, wallet chain, earring hanging from his left lobe but, oddly, no tattoos. He dangled the key out before him with the delicacy of a bear holding a China teacup.

"What the hell happened here?" he asked Adrianne.

"I have absolutely no idea," her voice was wispy with incredulity. "I was out from early yesterday until now." Then her voice cracked, "I . . . I had to go to my Dad's. He's, he's dead. He . . ." she fell into the warm bear hug that was Horse. He enveloped her like a mothering koala.

"Just hang in there, babe," he said. "You don't have to go into it. I'm here for you, so are Alice and everyone else. Take your time, there's no rush," he told her, as Rawlins fidgeted.

Adrianne once again had to pull it together. She sniffled and continued. Her voice gaining strength as she focused on the immediate devastation, putting her father's death out of her mind for the moment.

"I came in the back and found all this. Did you happen to hear or see anything yesterday, or last night?"

"Took Alice to the doc yesterday afternoon and then filled in for Barry at the bar from about eight 'til two this morning. Sorry."

"Is Alice all right?"

"Yeah, just an ear infection. Kid stuff. Doc gave us a 'script for Augmentin. She's startin' to feel better already. Anything I can do to help you here?"

"Thanks, I'll think of something. I've got a show to do for First Friday and a memorial to plan for my Dad."

"Just let me know," Horse said, as he took in the scene and then sized up Rawlins. "The doc's name is Lane, the bar is the Brewery II on Kalamath, between Third and Fourth," he told the sergeant, realizing she would want to check out his alibi. "At the doc's you'll want to ask about Eugene Spielberg and his daughter Alice. At the bar you can use either name."

Rawlins nodded once toward the uniformed officer who was standing by the door and taking notes.

Chapter 6

Adrianne twisted the key in the lock, let the door swing open, and stepped back to let the sergeant enter first. The upper level apartment took up a little more than half the area of the gallery below. It was a loft with the only apparent enclosed area being the bathroom. But it was fresh and new, unlike the stereotypical New York-style loft you see in movies. Yes, the east wall was exposed brick, and the ceiling was industrial steel with exposed ducts and pipes that were painted like a Georgia O'Keefe sky. But it also boasted vinyl-clad, double-pane windows and matching French doors that opened to the wrought-iron balcony we saw from the alley; and where I could see Adrianne's keys splayed out like a happy puppy on the wine-colored deck.

There was another large, newer window on the north wall that provided the ideal light for painting, and a third smaller one on the west wall that overlooked the front of the gallery below. The kitchen area had cabinets, a sink, dishwasher and refrigerator along the south wall. There was an island with drawers, a serving bar and a stove, over which hung a stainless steel circle from which dangled a colorful assortment of pots, pans and cooking utensils. All the countertops were a pinkish-brown granite.

The elegant and contemporary feel of the loft's finishes told me that Adrianne worked with professionals in the design and construction of the space. There was a room built into the southeast corner of the loft that was certain to be the bathroom. One of its walls was broken up by a large square of glass blocks that also served as the headboard for a queen-size bed. A couple of rolling clothes racks, apparently refugees from the garment district, served as an open-air closet The racks were festooned with a colorful array of slacks, tops, a few long dresses and, of course, jeans—many with paint stains. A cherry wood dresser for other things rounded out Adrianne's fashion corner. Not far from the bed were a couch, coffee table and chairs, where she could entertain or hang out and watch a 55-inch TV suspended off-center in a giant web of delicately thin aircraft cable that reached from the ceiling to floor and doubled as a room divider.

The flooring throughout was lacquered hardwood with an unusual inlay that I finally identified as recycled bowling alley lanes.

The remaining two-thirds of the loft was studio. Two *taborets* garnished with pigments, overflowing brush holders, colorful pallet knives and brightly speckled rags, stood guard next to a large easel whose most recent work had escaped to join its brethren in stacks leaning against any sturdy structure or immobile object around the loft. Obviously, Adrianne's recent energies were being diverted from creativity to commercialism, as she amassed her canvasses for their grand debut in little more than a week.

Rawlins and Adrianne were taking in the room bit-by-bit along with me. "What do you see?" the sergeant asked.

"Looks the same as usual," Adrianne said. "Can I use my bathroom for a minute?"

"Let's have a look first," Rawlins said as she led the way across the loft.

Despite the professional construction job, there were still a few places where the floor creaked underfoot. In the studio portion Adrianne allowed the floor to become freckled with a rainbow of paint dots—an acceptable occupational hazard.

Going from studio to living area was like jumping from the right brain to the left. Here things were orderly and tidy. In the bathroom there was an array of things on the counter yes, but cap on toothpaste, soap in holder, towels neatly hung, though not folded. A large tub shower with granite surround that matched the granite bathroom counter told me this lady was no starving artist. She indulged herself with carefully chosen luxuries.

"Looks fine to me," Adrianne said, now if you'll both excuse me," and she shut the only door in the loft.

***

The sergeant and I moved away from the bathroom toward the French doors. Rawlins twisted the deadbolt and opened one of the doors. We stepped out and she scooped up Adrianne's keys.

"So, I'm guessing you didn't search this place yesterday?" I asked Rawlins conspiratorially.

"Of course not. We didn't have probable cause. And, we didn't know what we should be looking for."

"But you have your suspicions?"

"We're always bothered when there's no suicide note. Meckler's financials all seem to be in order."

"Which one?"

"Both," she answered. "Both Adrianne's and Aaron's divorces were well over a year ago. And, other than those events, there are no recent catastrophes in his life or hers."

"Did you know his daughter's first one-woman show is here next Friday? And that Meckler was a partner in the gallery?" I asked.

"All the more reason for him not to commit suicide," she answered.

We came back inside and hovered around the coffee table as Adrianne rejoined us. "I heard you talking on the balcony," she said, as Rawlins handed over her keys. "You were talking about my father. What do you know?"

"Please sit down Ms. Meckler." Both women sat on the couch, a quarter turn toward each other. I took the chair.

"It wasn't a suicide, was it?"

"I'm beginning to think not. But we're not having any luck finding a motive for foul play, much less a suspect. We'll definitely keep you posted," Rawlins continued. "And, I'm sorry to say, we're sure to be back with more questions. In the meantime, is there anything I can do for you?"

"I'll need to know when I can have his body. Well, when the Neptune Society can have his body. It's Jewish tradition to bury someone within 24 hours," she said with more calm than I expected.

"I understand. But the medical examiner can't possibly finish the autopsy and reports that soon. But, I'll let them know and get back to you. I hope you and your rabbi will understand."

"I'm sure she will. But anything you can do will be appreciated. Oh, there is one more thing."

"What's that?" Rawlins asked.

"I know you have to look around here, take pictures and all. But, is there any way you can expedite that? I have my opening next week. I know it sounds petty under the circumstances . . ."

"I'll get the boys to take pictures and dust for prints as quickly as accuracy allows. Wren told me about your father's interest in the gallery. And I know from experience that diving back in is good therapy. We'll do what we can. Will you be all right?"

Adrianne said, "I think so. Horse and my other friends will pitch in. And Sebastian said he'll stick around to help. There might even be an article in it for him," she gave me a knowing look.

"Thought never crossed my mind," I said.

"We're good for the time-being," Rawlins said. "I'll get the crime scene guys out here. Don't touch anything downstairs until they give you the okay. But, call a locksmith to come out this afternoon to fix the front door. And get that burglar alarm installed A.S.A.P."

***

"You seem to be recovering a little," I said as soon as we heard the sergeant descending the stairs.

"In all honesty, I'm more than a little relieved that she's considering that it wasn't suicide. I hate to admit it, but I thought it might be my fault. Like maybe I spent too much time, or too much money, on the gallery."

"Rawlins told me on the balcony that your father's finances were all in order, so it wasn't the money. And I doubt there was anything you would have to be ashamed of."

"You never know," she deadpanned. "It's also the shock of the mess downstairs on top of everything else that is just numbing me out. When does this crap stop? Who would want to hurt my father and destroy my gallery? Why? This just doesn't make any sense."

Surprisingly, she didn't start to cry again, though her eyes were red as pomegranate skin and as watery as a sliced cactus.

"Didn't need to pee," she said.

"What?"

"When I went to the bathroom. I didn't need to pee. I went in to take some Prozac. I wanted it to kick in before the Valium I took this morning at your place wears off."

"That's how you kept your composure?"

"Yes. I took the coward's way out. Did you tell Rawlins about last night?"

"You're not being a coward. It's what those drugs are for. And no, I didn't see any reason to talk to her about how hard your father's death hit you. She knows."

"Not everything. The reason I tried to jump your bones last night . . ."

"You don't have to go there," I interrupted.

"I know. But you should know what you're getting yourself into. After Michael took everything and left, I tried to compensate by sleeping with anyone who would have me, you know, to feel that I was wanted. At least that's what I'm getting from therapy. I became a sex addict, though I didn't know it at the time. Didn't believe there is such a thing. The tipping point was when I met Mary Lou at a divorce support group. She was so nice and understanding. We had lunches, movies, dinners. We bonded. We bedded. We lived together for a few months. Then I found some letters she kept from previous lovers and realized it was her *modus operandi*. She would find vulnerable women at divorce groups and seduce them. Once again, I was a victim.

"I threw her out. First she tried to tell me how much I meant to her. Then she started to threaten me. But it's hard to threaten a woman in her own business about a same-sex relationship. Besides, who cares anymore? Especially in the art community—might even help."

I shifted in my seat at the bold mention of her lesbian affair, and then blushed at the way I had reacted.

"Relax Sebastian. I know it turns guys on. If you're thinking three-way, think about it with Michael instead of Mary Lou."

Touché, I thought.

"Or maybe Clive?" I went out on a limb.

"Oh, was that out loud?"

"I think you said, 'Where's Clive when you need him?'"

"No, I think I said, 'Where the hell is Clive when you need him.' Clive was another asshole that just wanted to take advantage. He promotes himself as a holistic healer and psychotherapist—you know you don't need a license in

Colorado to call yourself a psychotherapist?"

"Really? I know you need a license to cut hair. Wouldn't messing around inside someone's head be more important than trimming the outside?"

"Pretty messed up, isn't it. Well, I met Clive through a friend when I was still living in the suburbs. He kind of had an eleven-step program for addicts. Like AA minus Jesus, very whoo-whoo. I guess that's one of the reasons I'm telling you all of this. You know, the whole confession thing is one of the major steps. Anyway, long story short, he tells me that I'm having self-esteem issues. Duh. Then he convinces me that I'll feel better if we'd make love. But it was just his way of trying to control me. Afterwards, I felt like shit. I always felt like that afterwards.

"At that point I was feeling suicidal. Dad was very concerned and, for once, I listened to him. Without pressing me for details, he found a great psychiatrist and paid for some real therapy. Dr. Samuels prescribed the Prozac and helped me really regain my self-esteem."

"What happened to Clive?"

"I just told him to piss off. To get out of my life and to stop messing with people. He told me I had father issues and to just run back to Daddy. I was so angry, I threatened to press sexual harassment charges against a person in authority. I talked with Dr. Samuels about that, but she said that was almost exclusively to protect children. Also, as a consenting adult, it would be very hard to convict him of anything. And, most importantly, it would be better for my recovery to just let it go, Buddha-style.

"Anyway, that's all in the past. I'd been doing great for the past year. Cut back on the drugs, dealt with my emotions, poured myself into my work, took classes on Buddhism, Enneagram, Kabbalah. It's helping me to understand myself and rebuild. But yesterday was overkill. At your place the same old urge to just lose myself in someone else rushed back in like a tidal wave. I'm sorry to have put you through that. It won't happen again."

"Boy, that's a relief. I hate having a beautiful woman throw herself at me," I tried to lighten the moment.

The corners of her mouth dimpled slightly as she said, "You know what I mean."

I did. And it made me feel like an idiot for saying it.

Chapter 7

While the crime scene officers moved about downstairs doing that voodoo that they do so well, Adrianne and I busied ourselves with the tasks at hand. Her
 first order of business was to arrange a memorial for her father, Aaron Meckler. He had been a member of Temple Sinai for many years. So, while Adrianne called the rabbi, I volunteered to contact a security company to arrange for new locks and an alarm system for her gallery/home.

Since Aaron Meckler was a member of the Neptune Society, they said they would coordinate with the coroner to get his body, as well as for his cremation. "As a pragmatist and shrewd businessman, Dad always said burial plots are a waste of good real estate."

Fortunately, Temple Sinai is reformed; Orthodox Judaism doesn't allow cremation. Meckler's rabbi said she would arrange for an urn for the memorial, whether he had been cremated yet or not.

Since Aaron's house was still a crime scene, and AM Gallery was a disaster area—as well as a crime scene—it was decided that the memorial would be held at the temple Sunday afternoon, with the reception in the temple's hall afterwards. "Would you like me to call a caterer?" Rabbi Roberta Weisel asked.

"Let me get back to you," Adrianne said into the phone. "I want to check with the caterer I'm using for First Friday next week. She owes me a few favors."

Sitting at the dining table, Adrianne ended her phone call and filled me in on her progress. I sat on her bed, on hold with the security company my friend and neighbor Charles Love had recommended.

"We're going to have the memorial Sunday at Temple Sinai," Adrianne said, the progress of making arrangements improving her mood. "The rabbi also offered to arrange the catering for Dad's memorial."

"So the temple can mark up the price for the building fund?" I asked irreverently.

"Careful, lightning's going to strike." she answered. "But you know, Dad would never forgive me if I paid too much. I'm going to call Susan Glasscock; she's doing my opening next week, but I don't know if she does Jewish; or short notice.

"The rabbi's also going to post a notice on the congregation's website and arrange the obituary for tomorrow's paper so Dad's friends can come. I'm going to call a few of Dad's closest friends. That should get the word out pretty fast."

"I'm sure the legal grapevine is already burning up with the news. I'm surprised there hasn't been a story out on this yet. Sergeant Rawlins must be keeping a tight lid on it for now."

"I hadn't thought about that. You're right. I'm very grateful. Otherwise my phone would be ringing off the hook, and there'd be a rafter of reporters in front of the gallery," she smiled.

"Rafter? As in rafter of turkeys? Clever girl."

"Anyway," Adrianne continued, "Rabbi Weisel will do a great job. She's known Dad for years and she's an excellent speaker."

That's almost redundant, I thought, a religious leader being a good speaker. Then the security company rep came back on the line. I held up a finger and listened, confirmed the information and hung up.

"Security company should be here by four, and they'll call a half hour before to make sure someone's here. I gave them my cell 'cause I don't know your number. They're going to install a long metal plate on the door frame so this can't happen again. They're also going to install motion detectors, an audible alarm loud enough to scare the bejesus out of anyone within 100 feet of the building, as well as automatically notifying their call center."

"Is all that really necessary?" she asked.

"Jim Love thought a bit of overdoing would be a good idea for now, considering the break-in and the mystery surrounding your father's passing. If you think it's too much, you can back the system down later."

"He's right, I guess. Sounds like a good friend to have. Will you invite him and his wife to my opening next Friday? I'd like to meet and thank them in person."

"Sure thing."

"Anyway, I can't move the paintings down into the gallery until those guys are done and we've cleaned the place. It's just as well to have the paintings locked up in here. First thing I need to do is get more aircraft cable, some white Kilz to paint out the garbage they wrote," she was moving into the zone, not so much talking to me as thinking out loud. I just kept my mouth shut. "I think there's still enough hardware, or we can reuse the stuff from before, yeah, we really only need to replace the cables and paint out that filth."

She finished her thought and looked up, but was still having a debate with herself, "But I shouldn't leave here. They might come back. Shit. I don't want to be alone here. That's terrible. This is my home. I've poured everything I've got into it, financially and emotionally. It's a new and different way to be violated. What if they came back and I'm all alone? Maybe I can go to my father's . . . Oh God no, I can't stay there now."

"You have insurance?" I broke in.

"Uh, yes."

"Okay. Let's call your agent and find out what's covered. Damages for sure, but maybe money for a hotel and for a security guard."

"That's great Sebastian, I'll call her."

What seemed like a good idea at the time just added another layer of gray. Her insurance would pay for the lock repair and to replace the aircraft cables that had been cut by the vandals. Also, a couple of gallons of Kilz—a paint that covers over just about anything in one coat. Beyond that, nothing, *nada, nunca,* zero, the big bagel. Fat lot of good the insurance company is. They said that the structure, and in particular, the living quarters, had not been damaged. That the possibility of vandals returning were slim and not any of their corporate concern, not even with a police report. And, adding insult to injury, the repairs Adrianne noted were probably far less than the deductible, so she would be better off not even filing a claim.

"What about your friends in the neighborhood? Maybe Horse? Can you stay with one of them?"

"Oh, they'd make room. But it will be a hassle. Especially for Horse, he's living over his studio with his wife and Alice. It has less space than this."

"You could try a hotel, but you probably shouldn't be alone at a time like this," I said, trying to emphasize the death of her father and pending show, rather than the obscure possibility that someone was targeting her. "So, if Motley doesn't mind, you're welcome to stay at Chez Wren."

"You're too kind. I couldn't."

"Won't take no for an answer."

***

The afternoon was very productive. We left the crime scene in the very capable hands of Rawlins' investigators who said they would call when they were getting ready to leave. We grabbed a couple of delectable bagel sandwiches at Rosenberg's Deli in Five Points and then hit a giant warehouse in the heavy industrial section of Denver. It offered a huge, eclectic collection of small parts for machines, airplanes, boats, RVs; you name it. Although the place was crawling with men in coveralls and work apparel, she was greeted warmly by an old buzzard with flowing white hair and a beard—which partially concealed the oxygen tubes running from his regulator to his nose.

"Adrianne, how's the opening coming?" he barked over the heads of the men at his counter.

"Had a little setback, Mac. I'm going to need some more cable and stuff, grab me a number, willya?"

She picked up a shopping basket, handed it to me, and then worked her way through the maze of shelving, tables and bins like a super mouse going directly for the cheese. She made stops for the cable and cable crimps, along with other hardware that escaped my ken, and which she didn't take the time to explain.

In the midst of the musty warehouse her phone rang. It was Rawlins. We paused between a rainbow of spooled wire and a towering rack of shiny copper and aluminum pipes. She put her cell on speaker. "Wren's here too," she said.

"Good. Glad he's keeping you company. I'm sorry to have to tell you this over the phone, but the M.E. can't find any evidence to indicate your father's death was anything other than suicide."

"I understand," Adrianne said.

"But, I still have my doubts. From what you've told me, and what I know about attorneys and judges, something just doesn't smell right. Also, so far, we can't find anything that ties your father's death to the vandalism at your place last night, but we're not ruling it out either. I know I asked before, but can you think of anyone who would want to hurt you or your father?"

"No, sergeant, I can't."

"What about your ex-husband?"

"Figuratively, yes. In reality, no. He's a fast talker, not a murderer."

"You didn't think he was a con-man, either."

"Yeah, you're right."

"Did you mention Mary Lou or that guy Clive?" I said.

"Who?" Rawlins asked.

"A couple of acquaintances that might be pissed at me. Wait a sec, I'm going to take this off speaker so I can tell you more in private."

She finished her conversation with the policewoman and said, "Rawlins is going to check up on Mary Lou and Clive. But I don't think it's them. They barely knew my father, and I can't picture them committing a hate crime."

"A hate crime?"

"Rawlins thinks that maybe, since we're Jewish, and Dad was a prominent member of the community, and because of the anti-Semitic slurs on the hanging panels, it might just be some neo-Nazi crazies."

"A breaking-and-entering, maybe even vandalism," I said, "but murder? And nothing anti-Semitic at the townhome? I find that hard to believe. I doubt the two are a coincidence, but I can't think of a single thing that ties them together, except the timing."

"I have to agree," she said. "But it beats hell out of me what that might be. It seems Rawlins feels that way too."

"Did she say anything else?"

"Just that they finished the autopsy and called the Neptune Society to pick up his body. Oh, Sebastian, I should be there, not here buying all this stuff."

"There's nothing you can do there, Adrianne," I took her by the shoulders to indicate that if she needed a hug or a shoulder to cry on, I was available. "Didn't you say your goodbyes yesterday at his house?"

"Yes, but . . ."

"And you will do it again Sunday. There's plenty of time to grieve, believe me. But right now it's time to live. To accomplish what you and Aaron planned. You know in your heart, at least from what you've told me, that's what he would want."

Chapter 8

We got back to the studio around 3:30. The crime scene investigators were stowing the last of their gear in their vans. "We sent one of those hanging thingies back to our lab for further examination. We want to type the paint they used and test for other evidence," an officer told Adrianne. "We don't think it will really lead to anything, but we have to consider even the smallest details. Hope you don't need it for a while. We also found a pair of wire-cutters on the floor that the perp probably used to cut the cables. Hard yellow rubber handles, those yours?"

"Yes they are," Adrianne answered.

"You better get another pair, if you need them. They're coming down to the lab, too."

"How long will you need the wall and the cutters?" she asked.

"We only need them for a couple a days. But the D.A. will want them as evidence. So you won't get them back until after a trial. That could be more than a year." She nodded her understanding. "Hope this doesn't spoil whatever you had planned."

"The walls are part of the display for my work. I'm having a showing that starts next Friday. Thanks for not taking them all."

"Best of luck with your show," the inspector said with sincerity, then turned back to his van.

The police van was barely to the end of the alley when the front door filled with the specter of Horse again. "Good timing," Adrianne said, "I was just going to call you. I need another wall for my show."

He was followed into the gallery by another muscular man who was much larger than me, but nowhere near the size of Horse. "Dirt," he said, "that's Sebastian, a friend of Adrianne's. What size wall you need?"

"Good question, let's see what we have here. Sebastian, these guys can handle the display walls, but I was hoping you could stick around too."

"Sure. Let me make a few calls. I need to rearrange the interviews for my Holocaust article."

"Use my apartment upstairs. It might get noisy down here."

I went up to her place and started making calls while I nosed around. Occupational hazard? Bad habit? Or just inappropriate curiosity? Whatever. At first I just looked more closely at everything. Peeked at canvases that leaned casually but carefully against walls and other stable objects. Bright colors, flowers, abstracts. There was something very erotic about them. I liked almost everything, save one small canvas that looked like a child's attempt at a night sky festooned with oddly-colored stars orbiting what looked like a cluster of planets or other stars. I thought the show is going to be a great success, as long as she kept the starscape out of it. One by one, I postponed all of my scheduled interviews until the week after her opening.

I also took the liberty of calling the editor of an upscale art magazine and suggested an article on how gallery shows come together from a backstage perspective. He liked the idea. I felt like a pimp. But it's what I do.

Periodically I would walk over to the window that overlooked the gallery to see Horse and Dirt strenuously tilting the large display walls up onto a flat, carpeted dolly.

Then, under Adrianne's direction, carefully wheeling them over to lean against the exposed brick of the building. Noting that they were all engrossed in their work, I took the opportunity to revisit the bathroom and check the medicine cabinet. Aspirin, Prozac, antihistamine, naproxen, birth control pills, the usual array of makeup. There was a thermometer, bandages and tapes. Nothing nefarious in here, I thought.

Temptation got the better of me and I slowly eased open a dresser drawer. A quick peek made me blush as pink as one of the satin cords draped haphazardly over a purple plastic vibrator. I pushed the drawer back in as fast as silence allowed. I had gone far beyond propriety.

I took one more look through the window to the gallery to make sure my extra-curricular activities went unnoticed. I checked my complexion in the bathroom mirror hoping all telltale signs of my blush, and its guilty significance, had disappeared; then headed for the stairs.

"Can I help with that?" I asked from the stairway. They were upending the floating walls and placing them in a way where one could access both sides at once so they could be painted over. The cut cables from the vandalism hung down over the surface of the display walls like the tentacles of a dead squid. These had to be removed from eyehooks screwed into the two-by-fours at the top of the each wall.

I looked up and saw where matching cut cables dangled from the ceiling like the worn-out streamers of a lost political campaign. As my gaze came down I caught a glimpse of a man across the street who seemed to be looking too hard at the gallery. A large delivery van cruised by in traffic, and when it had passed, the man was nowhere to be seen. But the picture was etched in my brain; black turtleneck, or mock turtle, black pants and black leather jacket. But how unusual is that outfit in this day and age? Especially in the chill of autumn on gallery row? I chuckled at the recollection of myself in similar garb being mistaken for a Catholic priest at a former in-law's funeral.

We worked into the evening getting all the floating walls arranged and accounted for. The wall that was now in custody was, like most of its companions, four feet by eight feet. The security company people had come and gone, installing the additional steel plate to protect the doorframe, and keying a new lock to Adrianne's old key for convenience. Motion detectors snuggled into corners at both floor and ceiling levels. Hidden wires provided low-voltage electricity. Internal transponders communicated wirelessly to a surprisingly small panel in the back room. Wireless keypads had been installed at the rear entry and in Adrianne's apartment/studio upstairs. The head installer spent about a half hour with her going over how the very sophisticated system works, making sure she reset her passcode before he left.

Dirt left without so much as a goodbye, and Horse excused himself to go home to have dinner with his family, "I can come back later if you need more help," he said.

"No, thanks Horse. We've all done enough for one day. Just let yourself in tomorrow to build another four-by-eight."

"What about the alarm?" he asked.

"Call me when you get here, I can turn it on and off from my cell phone. Do you have all the materials you need?"

"I'll pick them up in the morning."

"Can you get another pair of wire cutters too. The vandals used mine and now the cops have them in custody."

"No problem. Where'll you be?"

"Sebastian's offered to let me crash in his guest room for a few days."

"Thanks man," he said to me, "take good care of her."

***

53

We had worked up an appetite that deserved the wonderful pasta served at Pasquini's, a few blocks from my townhome. The work had been good for both of us. It took Adrianne's mind off her father's death, at least for a little while. And for me, guilty as charged, I was making mental notes for what I hoped would be an article for that upscale art magazine.

I ordered a Vino Nobile de Montepulciano I recognized from a trip my late wife and I had taken to Italy. It was smooth and reasonably priced, though not the bargain it was in the town for which it is named. With the first glass I toasted, "To the memory of your father and the success of your show."

"That's very kind. There's still a lot to do. The vandalism set me back several days."

"At least you have this weekend. It would have been much worse next Friday."

"Are you always so optimistic?"

"Honestly, no. But I saw your work, I think it's wonderful. Horse seems dedicated to helping you. And I'll stick around to pitch in, if you don't mind? So I'm sure it will be ready in time."

"You're an art critic, too?"

"Not even close. But, would you mind a comment?"

"Just be gentle."

"There's a small starscape in your studio . . ."

She immediately burst into tears. I was flummoxed. I thought she was more confident about her work. Or would at least shine on any criticism this neophyte might broach.

"Adrianne, I'm so sorry. Don't pay any attention to my opinions on art. I'm a writer, what the hell do I know?"

She dabbed at her tears with her napkin. Other patrons were looking at us, trying to be politely discreet, but wondering what this oaf did to make this lady's eyes rain down tears.

Regaining her composure for the fifth or sixth time since we met, she said, "Actually, your taste is spot on," she sobbed and kind of laughed at the same time. "That painting is awful. But it isn't mine. My father painted it. He just did it in my studio one day a few weeks ago, while I was putzing around downstairs. He seemed very proud of it. He told me, 'whatever you do, don't sell this one.' I think he was just pulling my leg, but I certainly can't part with it now."

"Of course not."

"But crappy as it is, I think I want to display it at my opening."

"Why the hell not?" I said, adding lightly, "Just not in the front window." She lowered her eyes, smiled and nodded in agreement.

At that moment, our waiter approached with our dinners and I decided to try to change the subject, "So, what's Horse's story?"

"Just a big teddy bear," she said, leaning back to allow a plate of ravishing ravioli to go on the table before her.

"Just a big, intimidating teddy bear," I said. "And one with a record?"

"He got busted for having some pot."

"In this day and age?"

"Well, no. It was fifteen years ago and it was a little more than 'some.'"

"Now you know I have to ask."

"A hundred kilos."

"That's 2,200 pounds. A ton of weed is a little more than personal use, even for someone his size. How did he get out so soon?"

"He doesn't talk about it. But after he finally told me his real name, I did a little research and found out that shortly after his bust, a notorious drug gangster was arrested, tried on a number of counts, the least of which was bringing in truckloads of marijuana from Mexico—one of which I assume Horse was driving—and put away for about 100 years."

"And his name really is Eugene Spielberg?"

"You've got a good memory."

"He makes quite an impression. Any relation?"

"Doubt it. Or very distant."

"Now I know why someone that looks like him doesn't have any visible tattoos."

"Exactly. He's not a very religious Jew, but you know, there are some traditions that transcend lifestyle choices."

"He doesn't keep kosher, does he?"

"No way," she laughed.

We finished our raviolis and eggplant parmesan, along with the bottle of wine, and headed back to my place.

"If you don't mind," she yawned, as she slogged up the stairs to the guest room carrying a bag of things she brought from her place.

"Not at all. Sleep well, I know I will."

Chapter 9

I was true to my word. I was sleeping soundly until I heard Janis Joplin belting out "Take Another Piece of my Heart"—an unfortunately appropriate ring tone for Adrianne's phone. It was 12:14, according to my clock.

"This can't be happening," I heard her voice go off like a geyser. A moment later, she threw open the door to my bedroom, sending Motley scurrying for cover in the open closet. She was wearing a white, long-tail, V-neck, T-shirt.

"What? What?" I stammered.

"Someone heard gun shots on Santa Fe," her voice snapped like a bullwhip. "The police came and there was a fire at the gallery. They put it out with extinguishers from their cars. They said it was small. Sebastian, I gotta go." She disappeared back into the guest room.

I swung out of bed in my briefs and slid on jeans, socks, boots and grabbed a T-shirt as I flew down the stairs. She was a nanosecond behind me, still in the white T, but with jeans and flip-flops. "Better grab a sweater or a jacket," I reminded her, pulling a shirt over my head. I gathered my pocket paraphernalia and slipped into my coat.

By 12:50, Adrianne and I were standing in front of the gallery. Although the harmless flames had been put out half an hour earlier, firemen were still scrutinizing the scene.

"I don't understand what happened," we heard a fireman telling the police officer in charge. "Why would anyone throw a kerosene lamp at the stone façade, and not through the window?"

The police were also looking over the scene. Adrianne and I came in closer and identified ourselves to the police. "You made it here in record time," the officer in charge said. "Apparently someone tossed a Molotov cocktail at your gallery. But all they did was heat up the wall below the window. Either he didn't have much of a throwing arm, or he has an agenda we've never seen before. Or, he could have been drunk."

"What about the gun shots?" Adrianne asked, as I took a closer look at the burn area.

"Not sure," the officer said. "That was just what was reported. And, to clarify, it was just one shot. A sound like that can come from any number of things: a car backfiring, a firecracker, a board falling flat."

"Is this related to what happened last night?" Adrianne asked, her voice quaking with fear and anger.

I noticed a scratch mark on the slate below one of the large plate glass windows. I didn't remember seeing it earlier. I looked up across the street. Lights were on in the upper windows in several buildings. But the one that stood out was dark. It was were a movement caught my eye; black on black, shadow against shadow. Then it was gone. I chose not to say anything.

"Two nights in a row, two incidents at the same address?" the officer said. "We can't call that a coincidence, Ms. Meckler. Even though they're very different in nature, we gotta keep an open mind about it. Would you mind if we looked around inside?"

"Not at all. It would make me feel much better," a modicum of calm returning to her voice. She unlocked the front door, turned off the new alarm, and let the two policemen enter.

She came back out and waited with me outside until the

police checked the main level. They came and got Adrianne so she could let them into her studio and apartment. Although it was a wide open space, the officers took ten minutes to closely examine everything, double-checking the lock on the balcony door, looking under and behind anything that had an under or behind.

They gave her the all clear and an unnecessary admonition to call if there was any more trouble. They said a detective from the department would be by in the morning to get a statement, and then left. It was 1:45.

As soon as they were gone I asked if she had a flashlight. We took it outside and I lighted up the scratch on the slate just below the window. "Isn't this stonework new?"

"Yes. Dad had it done about a month ago. He never would have approved a piece with an imperfection like that. Maybe some kid on a skateboard, or the guy with the chisel from last night. Who knows?"

As she spoke I looked along the sidewalk until I found what I suspected, a mash of lead that still had a cylindrical shape at one end. "I'm no expert," I said. "But I think this could be a spent bullet. If it made that scratch and ended up here, it might have been fired from up there," I pointed to the dark window where I thought I'd seen movement earlier. "It could have hit the sidewalk, ricocheted against the slate and tumbled down here."

She followed my gaze and, like the last leaf of autumn falling quietly on the grass, said, "That's Horse's place."

I stayed with the untouched bullet fragment while Adrianne went up to her apartment to get a plastic bag and a paper towel. While she was gone, I used my phone to take a picture of the bullet, the scarred slate, a mark in the sidewalk that might have been the point of impact—it was hard to tell with all the pockmarks and chewing gum residue—and a couple of photos encompassing all three points.

When she returned, I used the paper towel to pick up the

bullet and dropped it in the plastic sandwich bag she held
open.

Feeling like real detectives, we were so focused on our
work we didn't hear anyone approaching until the man said,
"I wouldn't bother with that."

The voice was soft but commanding. We both turned
expecting to be looking at a formidable weapon. It was
Horse. "Can we go inside and talk about this?" he asked.
"The cops will certainly be driving by more often than usual,
and I'd rather not be involved."

Adrianne led the way with Horse following. I twisted the
deadbolt in the front door. We went up to her studio
apartment. She turned on only one torchiere light that
bounced off the cloudy New Mexico sky of her ceiling,
providing a soft, warm illumination for the whole place.
"Anyone else want some coffee or tea?" she asked.

"Some decaf for me, if you have it," I said.

"If you got any mild Celestial Seasonings . . ." Horse
requested. "Been a long night. Gotta take the kid to school in
the morning, I'd like to get some sleep sometime."

"What's happening, Horse?" Adrianne asked while she
tended to drinks in the kitchen.

"That bullet," he began, "it's mine." His statement didn't
surprise me, Adrianne or any other sentient life form. "We
were in bed reading and she got up to pee. The window was
open, you know how she likes the fresh air, even on cold
nights."

"She?" I asked.

"My wife, Darlene. Anyway, she was coming to bed when
she saw a car pull up in front of your gallery. She thought
she saw a man lean out the window and try to light
something with a match. After last night, she was very
concerned and told me to come look. I grabbed my .38 from
the night stand and sure enough, the sonofabitch had gotten
out of the car, set a little lamp thing on the roof and was

lighting the wick. I was going to run down and stop him, but he picked it up and cocked his arm. I knew I couldn't get there in time, so I shot him."

"You shot him?" Adrianne asked, stunned.

"Well I tried. I don't know if I hit him, or if I just scared the hell out of him. But that arm just didn't complete its arc. That's why the lamp hit below the window. I'm sure he wanted that thing to go through it.

"Anyway, I knew the gun shot would bring the cops, so I ducked back into our room and turned off the lights. The little bastard just melted back into his car and drove off. The cops were here within three minutes. And they had that little fire out in another two. I guess that's when they called the fire department and, probably, you."

"You didn't call the cops, did you?" I asked.

"No way. Musta been someone else in the neighborhood who didn't want to get involved."

The banshee whistle of the tea kettle demanded Adrianne' attention. She turned off the gas and poured hot water into three cups. I asked Horse, "What did this guy look like?"

"Well. He was crouched, so it's hard to say how tall, but maybe five-nine. He looked slender, but he was wearing all black. He had very blonde hair, that was easy to see, even at night. You know him?" he asked, as Adrianne brought the cups out all at once, waitress style.

"Think I've seen him," I said, sipping a cup of instant decaf that tasted like a soggy brown-paper bag.

"Who is he?" Adrianne asked, I noticed she had opted for tea.

"I didn't want to alarm you, but I think I saw someone who meets that description yesterday while we were straightening up downstairs. But, except for that bright blonde hair, there are hundreds of men who are about five-nine with a slight build and wear dark colors."

"Yeah, I know. I was married to one. Well, his hair was a

very light brown, but in certain lights . . ."

Horse and I just stared at her.

"What, you don't think it could have been Michael Stark? He'd never have the balls to do something like that."

"That's what they all say," Horse said.

"Well, we'll have to give the police the bullet and tell them what happened tomorrow," I said.

"Yeah, sure," Adrianne threw me a deprecating look. "Here, Horse," she handed him the sandwich bag with the bullet fragment, "finders keepers. If they missed it, then it's ours."

At first, I didn't like what she was doing. But I began to see the sense in it. Trying to stop the arsonist—and succeeding to a great extent—Horse had little if any bearing on the situation. Telling them about it would have them jumping to conclusions like a kangaroo on a hot beach. Better to keep it to ourselves, at least for the time being, I thought, remembering his little problem with a ton of pot.

Adrianne showed Horse out as I surreptitiously dumped the instant coffee in the kitchen sink. "Under the circumstances," she said when she came back upstairs, "I think it would be better if I stay here tonight."

"You're not afraid he might come back and try to burn you out?"

"Hell yes, I'm afraid. You would be too, if you have any sense. But the cops will be on extra patrols. He'd have to be an imbecile to come back tonight."

"I may not have any sense, but, if you'd like, I can stay. However, I won't be insulted if you want me to leave."

"Oh I'm sure you have good sense, Sebastian," she said as she came right up to me, but not in a needy or wanting way. "Actually, I was hoping you would stay."

"Is that a good idea?" I asked.

"I think so. After two full days together, under what I hope are the worst circumstances of my life, I think I'm getting to know the real you, and . . . "

"And?"

"And, you seem like a very sincere person to whom I am attracted and who I think is attracted to me, too."

"You're right about the second part. But, I'm really sorry, I have to ask . . ."

"No, godamnit, it's not the addiction talking," she turned away and walked over to the couch. "I'm sorry I tried that. I'm sorry I have a problem. I'm sorry I ever told you about it," her voice taut as violin strings. And then, softly, in retreat, in full surrender, "Just go. I understand."

I went over and guided her gently down to the couch where I sat beside her. "I'm sorry," I said. "I don't know enough about your problem to say the right things. You're a beautiful woman. That's easy to see. But, as you said, after the last two days, you appear even more beautiful inside than out. I don't know that I could ever expose my predilections and addictions as bravely as you did."

"But, you're not sure whether or not you're just a shot of whiskey for an alcoholic," she said, looking down at her lap.

"I wasn't sure before, but I think I know the answer to that now. May I stay?"

She raised her head, looked at me through watery eyes, smiled, raised one hand to my cheek and kissed me. "Please stay, Sebastian. But maybe you're right. Would you mind the couch? It folds out into a pretty good bed."

Chapter 10

Sunlight filtered through the shears Adrianne had drawn over the windows and French doors. There was a buzzing sound like bees in summer that made its way into the studio apartment. But it wasn't summer.

Adrianne bounced up like a well-oiled catapult. The blankets and sheet falling away from her. "What the . . ." Then she fell back and pulled the covers up to her chin.

"What?" I asked from my fold-out lair several feet away.

"It's just Horse," she said. Then I realized the buzzing was the sound of someone cutting lumber below us in the gallery, muffled by the sturdy, locked door of the apartment. "I guess we should be getting up. There's lots to do, beginning with . . . ," she bounded out of her bed heading straight for the bathroom while revealing a pair of lime green panties below her T-shirt. The door closed and I lay in bed quietly, wishing I had gotten there first. That said, she was considerate enough to make it short and offered me the facilities.

"How did he get in with the alarm set?" I asked.

"I texted him the code before we went to bed. It was another long hard day and I didn't know how late we might sleep. I need to get new walls built. The others need cleaning, painting and hanging. And then there's the art. It can't just go anywhere, you know."

We were downstairs within a half hour. In one hand I

held a breakfast burrito that had made the journey from *bodega* to freezer to microwave. In the other I was balancing an excellent cup of coffee made from fresh ground beans—a gigantean improvement from last night's instant decaf.

Adrianne descended the stairs with two empty cups, a carafe of coffee and two more burritos for Horse. He stopped his work and said, "Oh, sorry, hope I'm not too early."

"No problem," she said. "Here. A couple of Rosario's homemade burritos and some fresh brewed Costco."

"High test?"

"Of course."

Horse accepted the offerings and leaned back on a sturdy sawhorse to enjoy. "I'll be done cutting on the two-by-fours in a few minutes. After we sweep up, we can start painting over that crap on the other walls. This one should be done by the time those are painted." He obviously knew his way around construction and how to schedule a job.

"Just the three people we want to talk to," Detective Sergeant Rawlins said as she came through the unlocked front door. "Heard we had some excitement again last night."

"Good morning detective," Adrianne greeted her. "Care for a cup of coffee?"

"No thanks, I'm good."

The next hour was taken up with everyone stating where they had been last night, and what they were doing. We left out the part about Horse shooting at the amateur arsonist, but covered the description of the creep with my sighting of what could have been the same man lurking—well, I embellished a little—across the street yesterday afternoon.

"That isn't much to go on," Rawlins said. "But we've worked with less. We can't connect any dots between your father's place and the two incidents here, but we surely aren't ruling out the possibility. All three of the people you mentioned, your ex—Michael Stark, your other ex—Mary

Lou Webb, and, of course, the pseudo shrink—Clive Graber––are all still in the area and on our radar."

"On your radar?" I asked.

"Stark has been indicted and acquitted of running cons on two other women since Ms. Meckler. Webb has a restraining order against her for sexually harassing both members of a couple that had split up and then gotten back together. And Graber served a minimal term in county for sexual assault by a person in a position of authority. You sure know how to pick them, honey," the detective said. "Well, we have everything we came for. Besides, it looks like you have a ton of stuff to do before next Friday. We'll leave you to your work."

She turned toward the door and Adrianne matched her steps to see her out. "Have all the funeral arrangements been made for your father?" Rawlins asked.

"Rabbi Weisel's taking care of the memorial and the gathering afterwards at the temple," Adrianne said. "I'm hoping that the caterer doing my opening will handle the memorial as well. I've got a simple black dress and some pearls. I just have to organize my thoughts for a eulogy."

"The rabbi, is that Roberta Weisel?"

"Yes, you know her?"

"Yeah. A good woman. You know, you don't have to speak at the memorial, people will understand."

"You think it's okay?"

"I just said so. Is there anyone else in the family? Or close friends?"

"Dad has a cousin in Littleton. They've sort of drifted apart, but they grew up together. He's a nice guy. Maybe he'll say a few words."

"Give him a call. I'm sure he'll do well. Meanwhile, stay busy with these characters; it's probably the best medicine. Oh, by the way ..." Rawlins' voice trailed off as the two women crossed the threshold, walked over to where the police car was parked, talked for a few more minutes, shared a laugh, and then the detective drove off.

Adrianne reentered the gallery with a broad smirk, just as Horse looked up from his work.

"Something funny?" the big man asked.

"She thinks you're cute," Adrianne said.

"What?"

"While she was checking on Michael, Mary Lou and Clive, she checked on you two, too. She knows about your pot bust. Talked to narcotics and understands what went down. And, that it was 20 years ago and you have no record before or after."

"And, it's legal now, so who cares?"

"Certainly not me. But they still don't consider a ton of weed in a step van as just personal use," Adrianne said.

"What about me?" I asked, full of curiosity to know what the local *polizia* had on a hardworking journalist.

"Sorry Sebastian, you're just not on law enforcement's radar."

"Damn. And I really tried."

"With protests and sit-ins? She said you were a pussy cat. But, she thinks you might have potential in other areas," her eyes and smile lighting up like she'd just been included in MoMA.

"Should I start painting these guys?" I motioned toward the display walls, trying to ignore whatever innuendo the women shared.

"That would be great," Adrianne said. "Grab that can of Kilz Horse has been stirring. Don't be stingy with the paint, these things have to be pristine white. Try not to get any on you."

I looked down at my Levi's. They were new enough to pass for "Aspen Formal" and I didn't want to mess them up.

Adrianne saw my concern and said, "You might want to do a quick run over to your place if you have something better for this work. I'd loan you a pair of mine, but there's no way you could get into them, so to speak. And Horse, well, never mind."

"Be back in an hour," I said.

On the drive back to my place Nina Simone serenaded me with "Feeling Good," which I was. I had work to do on the Holocaust survivors, and I needed to stay sharp and keep the other piece I was planning on the backstage work of producing an art exhibit in mind. But I liked having a little change from interviewing, researching and writing. It was nice to just swing a brush, push a roller or drive in some screws with the camaraderie of artists like Adrianne and artisans like Horse.

But as Nina's song segued into BB King's "Everybody's Had The Blues," I started thinking a little more objectively about everything going on around me. It was good, I suppose, that Adrianne could put aside the death of her father and the vandalism on her gallery, for intermittent moments. The thought that I might be part of her coping mechanism didn't set well with my ego. The thought that the three incidents, or even two, were unrelated, didn't set well either.

As soon as I got home I called my friend Charles Love. "I'm here, man," he said when I asked about his location. "You wanna come over? Terri's got some stuff from the bakery and the coffee's still hot."

I had come in from the garage and, much to the chagrin of my cat, Motley, just walked through my house, out the front, down the sidewalk and turned up the path to the Loves' townhome. The computer maven and ex-Palm Springs cop, and his charming wife, had been friends for years. My late wife Heidi and I would take summer trips with them, and they were there for us through Heidi's leukemia, her death, and my recovery. You couldn't ask for better people.

"What's up?" the big black man greeted me. "You

sounded disconcerted."

"Perfect word for it."

"Come on in. Coffee?"

"Sure." I followed him into the kitchen.

"Hi hon," Terri greeted me. She was working on something with flour and butter and the last of the season's fresh peaches from Colorado's Western Slope. My hope was one of her remarkable pies crammed full of fruit and light on the sugar. I went around the center island and gave her a kiss hello before joining Charles at the table.

Over coffee and rugelach I told Charles that we hadn't been completely forthcoming with the police. That we held back some information, but didn't think we hurt the case. All the same, I wanted to find out more.

"Tell me what you got."

I described what had been going on with the death of Aaron Meckler, the vandalism at Adrianne Meckler's AM Gallery, and the mysterious man with Johnny Winter hair and Johnny Cash clothes. I covered every detail, including Horse shooting at the man with the lighted kerosene lamp; Charles did IT work for the Denver PD, had very high clearance, and had been—but wasn't—a cop.

"That's all of it?" Charles asked, it was a professional reflex, not an implication that I held anything back.

"Yep. That sums it up."

"Except for the thing between you and the girl," Terri said, rolling out dough. To my guilty look she said, "You ain't as much the Good Samaritan you might want us to think you are, Sebastian Wren. You got something going on in your head about that girl. But it's probably not germane to her daddy's passing or that other stuff with her studio," she grinned her blessing.

"Who's working it for DPD?" Charles ignored his wife's ribbing.

"Detective Sergeant Rawlins."

"Julie or Frankie?"

"Don't know, must be Julie."

"Five-eight, hundred-eighty-pound white guy?" Charles asked.

"The five-eight is right, but we're talking hundred-thirty-pound black woman."

"That's Frankie."

"But, Julie?"

"Short for Julius. Either way, they're both very good. I can have a look at her online file to see if there's anything there that might help you."

"Great. Give me a call."

Chapter 11

The Loves and I chatted through two more pastries and the rest of my coffee. I told them I'd be spending the rest of the day at Adrianne's studio, helping out. Terri said if I and "my lady friend" would like to join them for a casual dinner later, to let her know. Charles promised to look into Aaron's and Adrianne's strange cases, as much as propriety allows, and get back to me. No need to mention that no one was to know from whom the information came.

Since showering before schlepping display walls seemed futile, if not counter-productive, I spent the next half hour helping the neglected Motley cat get some exercise.

I brushed my teeth, changed into grubbies and packed a small bag with a change of clothes and a few essentials. I drove back to Adrianne's, but left my traveling bag in the car, not really knowing where I was going to spend the night. And not wanting to be too presumptuous. Besides, she was supposed to be staying at my place.

The rest of Saturday was mostly spent with Horse. For a few hours Horse's sphinx-like coworker, Dirt, was there too. He wandered in like a specter and disappeared as fast as a politician's campaign promise. The two large gentlemen decided the best use of their time was cobbling together the one wanting wall display and getting all of the panels hung where dangling cables indicated they had been. Covering the drywall screws with "mud," sanding and painting could all be done when the panels were in place; meaning by a relatively scrawny itinerant journalist.

Adrianne lent a hand wherever her small frame allowed. She would run upstairs from time to time, look at artwork, come back down and—without explanation—have the men relocate a display panel. She made more notes about the layout and nodded her approval as she visualized her artworks in their proper places.

Her supervision was constantly being interrupted by friends and family calling from as far away as the coasts. The first few calls elicited watery eyes and a sniffle or two. But after the sixth or seventh, while always being gracious, she seemed relieved to get off the phone and back to work. Her greatest comfort came just before noon when Susan Glasscock, her caterer, finally called back to tell her she would do the gig on Sunday, not to worry, and that she would coordinate with the rabbi. Susan also told Adrianne that she would do it at cost, as she didn't like profiting from the grief of her regular clients and friends.

One o'clock arrived with the delivery pizza and sodas. "You guys are doing great," the boss lady said, "but we need to get these things hung, mudded and painted by the end of the day. I want them to dry thoroughly tomorrow and then I can start hanging canvases Monday." She allowed herself to omit any mention of the next day's memorial. "I'll spring for beer when we're done, but I don't want anything to slow us down now."

After lunch, Adrianne disappeared upstairs. We had no immediate questions as she had marked the approximate height for each panel we were hanging on masking tape on the floor below where they would float, along with their bounty of art.

Occasionally, we heard her phone ring and her unintelligible, muffled conversation—more sympathies and condolences. I figured she would be resting after the past 48 hours of nonstop catastrophes and the physical and emotional toll it was taking on her. However, about 3:00, she called to me from the top of the stairs. I entered her apartment not knowing what was next.

"I'd like you to hear what I've written for my father's memorial tomorrow."

"Didn't the rabbi say she'd do the eulogy?"

"Yes, but I want to say some things she can't cover. If I can get through this a few times without breaking down, I think I'll be able to do it okay tomorrow."

We spent most of the next hour going over what she had written. It was from the heart and beautiful. When she stumbled over a phrase here and there, I helped her smooth it out so it flowed better, always keeping it in her voice. She practiced it out loud several times.

Between "takes" we chatted about the memorial arrangements, progress with the show setup downstairs, and a bit more about my background, especially how I coped with Heidi's passing. I also mentioned that if she was up for meeting new people, Charles and Terri Love had invited us over for a bite. She liked the idea.

She had no plans beyond the Friday night show. I was concerned for her, but beyond telling her to call if there was anything else I could do for her, I didn't have the necessary training or intuitive insight to really offer solace.

Before returning to the work in the gallery, she held up two hangers. One had a simple black dress. The other a black pantsuit. "What do you think?"

"The dress looks too formal. The neckline too revealing. The pantsuit is simple and elegant. A bright-colored blouse or maybe a silk camisole would relieve some remorse from the memorial, and make it more a celebration of Aaron's life, like the eulogy you wrote."

"Wow, where did that come from? Not some guy swinging a hammer downstairs."

"My mother was a clothing designer. When I was a kid, I

knew more about women's clothing than men's. Of course, all I needed to know was jeans and a clean shirt."

"I hope that's not what you're going to wear tomorrow. You are coming tomorrow, aren't you?"

"Yes, of course. And don't worry, I have a pair of formal black Levi's," I mocked.

"You wouldn't dare ..."
I realized she was truly concerned and put aside my tendency to tease, "Don't worry, I've learned to dress appropriately." She looked truly relieved.

***

I returned to the labor downstairs. Horse and Dirt had made great strides in my absence, or maybe because of it. Of the 13 panels floating strategically about the studio, only five needed to be rehung—including the one that needed to be built from scratch. I started painting out the various obscenities on two of the panels that had been defaced, but not cut down. By the time I got to a newly hung panel, Horse had painted two more, and Dirt had vanished.

It looked like we would be finished with the painting around half-past six. I gave Terri a call at Chez Love to let her know Adrianne and I would be taking her up on her invitation. As Horse and I were tamping down lids on paint cans, Adrianne appeared fresh from a shower with three open bottles of Fat Tire ale.

"We can leave the rest of the cleanup until tomorrow afternoon or Monday," she said, handing each of us a bottle. It was cold, wet, delicious and refreshing. "Do you want to shower here?"

"No thanks. It'll be easier at my place. Besides, I need to feed and pamper Motley."

"Maybe I can help with that." I wasn't sure if she was talking about the shower or the cat.

Chapter 12

Unfortunately for me, Adrianne had been referring to the cat. Dinner at the Loves' was Terri's gourmet gumbo that she makes in huge batches and freezes. She adds fresh shrimp when the Cajun concoction is at full boil, then turns off the heat, and waits 10 minutes, cooking the shrimp to perfection. Terri ladled the gumbo over bowls of brown rice. A flute of fresh French bread, butter and a good table red transported our palates to New Orleans.

Talk naturally went to the mysterious death of Aaron Meckler and the vandalism that punctuated the entire palette of incidents that plagued Adrianne the last few days. To avoid reliving every minute detail of the ordeal, she asked the Loves about themselves and some pointed questions about me. While flattering, it also caused me some discomfort. I tried to steer the conversation to the opening of the AM Gallery on Friday.

"I hope the two of you can come," Adrianne implored her hosts.

"We'd love to see your work," Terri answered. And the conversation moved easily on to art and some of the museums we collectively visited, both in the US and abroad.

It was an early evening as Adrianne and I had been working all day. Tomorrow was the funeral, and she was worn out, emotionally as well as physically.

Throughout the evening I had the feeling Charles wanted

to talk with me alone. He started to broach something when Adrianne went to the bathroom. But she returned sooner than anticipated and he segued over to his impressions of Picasso's very early, very traditional, works.

"I hate to be a wet blanket," Adrianne turned to Terri, "but it's been a hell of few days. And tomorrow I have to bury my Dad. Thank you for a wonderful dinner and for helping to take me away from my problems for a few hours. Sebastian, if you want to stay, I'm fine going back to your place and curling up with Motley."

"You can have dibs on Motley, but I'm not letting you walk home alone. Even if it's only a few doors away."

We all got up and walked to the front door. Hugs were exchanged all around and Charles whispered in my ear, "FaceTime me later." I nodded as Adrianne and I left.

Adrianne left her door ajar so Motley could come and go as his precious self desired. I went downstairs and brought my iPad back to my bedroom, passing the door to the guest room twice and hearing the soft breathing signs of sleep from within, punctuated by a soft, but unladylike snore or two.

I quietly closed the door to my bedroom hoping the cat didn't want in, and make a racket trying to get his way. I plugged in my earbuds and called Charles.

"That didn't take very long," he signed on.

"She's exhausted. I'm not feeling all that spry myself. Thanks for inviting us over. It really helped her, and well, anytime your lovely wife wants to pamper me with her cooking . . ."

"Yeah, got that."

"So what's up?"

"Like I told you, I did some, ah, research," meaning he accessed some files he shouldn't be looking at. "Anyway, I found out your Detective Rawlins is looking at four possible suspects for the mischief at the gallery. Well, for the torching attempt anyway, since that's the only incident where there's a perp's description. Her focus is on four men who come close to matching the guy you and your friend Horse described. They're David Perlstein, Percy Claude Chaffee, Leland Elroy, and Jody Kapp. Any of those names mean anything to you? Or could any of those names have come up when you and Adrianne were talking?"

I thought for a moment, just in case. "Nope."

"Not surprised, just had to ask. Maybe her father knew one of them?"

"If so, we'll probably never know."

"Not so fast, Kimosabe. Since Rawlins had run checks, we know a little about each of them. And, their last known addresses."

"You look like you're about to give me a present."

"Who knows? And, be careful what you wish for. Perlstein and Kapp are both currently in prison. Kinda lets them off the hook. Elroy's last known address is in Delta over on the Western Slope. Doesn't put him far enough away to not be a player, just makes Percy Claude Chaffee, or PC, as he likes to be called, a more viable suspect."

"So, where's our friend PC living?"

"According to his parole records, he's got a little place in Lakewood. Very convenient, wouldn't you say? And, you'll love this, he was recently paroled from the Englewood prison."

"That's where Aaron Meckler did mentoring. Can you make it any easier?"

"It's all just circumstantial, my friend."

"What's Rawlins and DPD doing about it?"

"All that the law and the weekend allow. They've sent emails to Elroy's and Chaffee's parole officers in Delta and Lakewood, with CC's to the Sheriffs in both Delta and Jefferson Counties."

"And they've heard . . .?"

"Like I said, it's the weekend. They've heard nothing, yet. And, as far as your next question, DPD is reluctant to try and get a warrant at this time."

"Because they only have a vague description of a man that could fit a few hundred other men, and one of the witnesses is a biker with a pissant record."

"That's only conjecture," Love said.

"You'd make a good diplomat."

"And a mediocre cop. I'm gonna email you the one-sheets on Elroy and Chaffee."

"Thanks, I'll look at them tomorrow when Adrianne isn't around. Right now I'm just too damn tired to do much of anything."

I closed the cover on my iPad and lay down on my bed. I was about to drift off when I remembered to open my door so the cat could wander about without waking me, or Adrianne in the next room.

Chapter 13

Stiff whiskers brushed my face and ended my slumber. "Time to feed me," his Motleyness entreated. My house guest seemed to still be sound asleep. My clock read 7:14. The memorial wasn't until 1:00. More than enough time for us to get ready. More than enough time for Adrianne to contemplate the day ahead. I thought it best to let her sleep.

Though a large cat, Motley had a very small voice, which he didn't even use this morning, perhaps in deference to his recent bedfellow. I put some food down for him, changed his water and cleaned his box. Having gotten Motley's priorities in order, I started to root around for some ground coffee that was a gift and had been stashed in my freezer since last Christmas. It would have to do, as I didn't want to run the grinder. Buttered toast with Oregon Marionberry jam sated my appetite without making noise or wafting breakfast smells up to Adrianne's room.

Sitting down to my continentalish breakfast, I plugged in my earbuds again and opened my iPad. My music mix brought up Judy Collins singing Donovan's "Sunny Goodge Street," which naturally had to segue into some Mingus, mellow fantastic. I went to the email from Charles and looked at the one-sheets for PC Chaffee and Leland Elroy. One-sheets, the modern day equivalent of a wanted poster: picture full-face and side, obligatory number and name, both candidates easily matched the description given by Horse and myself.

The photos were captioned with an overview of their nefarious deeds.

I expected, or hoped, to see that either or both had something very telling; an arrest for arson, membership in the Aryan Nations, activist NRA member, attempted murder, merit badge for tying knots—in particular a hangman's noose. Nothing, nada, zero, zilch, the big bagel. They were both petty criminals. Elroy arrested several times and successfully prosecuted for stalking when he was an older teenager and, as an adult, selling stolen goods. Chaffee was more interesting. His malevolent maraudings were more like a felonious chameleon. Maybe he believed in the old adage, "If at first you don't succeed . . ." As an adolescent, he stole cars. Parting them out without knowing how many different places manufacturers stamped vehicle identification numbers. Out of jail after a first-offense, 18-month sentence, he turned to cigarettes; no ID numbers, tremendous mark-up, addicted clientele—including undercover cops. He didn't know that in addition to selling goods, he was guilty of tax evasion. Paroled after three years, this time, he turned to burglary, but, without a thorough understanding of silent alarm systems. That earned him nine years at Englewood Prison, out in six with time off for good behavior. Just two months ago.

The same prison where Aaron Meckler had mentored inmates. Coincidence? I smelled a rat.

I had to visit this guy. Maybe I could pull a ruse by using my journalist's credentials. Story about prison conditions, or some such nonsense. He didn't seem like the brightest pixel on the screen. I was fairly confident he would want the 15 minutes of fame he thought a reporter might bring him.

I googled the address on his sheet. An old section of Lakewood where houses were small and far apart. Many had pretty good acreage. The satellite view showed several

Chapter 14

"You mean he committed suicide?" I asked the woman.

"No, no. Of course not."

"But, you're telling me that's what the police think?"

"Yes. But they're wrong. They're wrong. I know they are." Her voice was rising in anguish and anger.

A few people turned our way. I grabbed her arm again and pretty much shoved her out of the reception hall. Standing across from the restrooms, and still holding her left arm, I pulled her around with my other hand to face me. "I'm sorry for your loss, but please calm down. What you're saying isn't going to make it any easier for Ms. Meckler. We can talk. But you can't burden her with your story right now; not here."

I seemed to be getting through to her. I realized she had been shaking and was beginning to relax. "Please Mrs. . . ."

"I go by Brown. Elizabeth Brown. My husband was Marvin Saines. I kept my maiden name for my career. Marvin was fine with it. Marvin was fine with a great number of things," her voice dropped and her eyes watered.

"Ms. Brown, my name's Sebastian, Sebastian Wren. Can I get you something? A glass of water, or wine?"

"Thank you," she looked down and then looked up quizzically. "Do they have wine here?"

"Of course, it's tradition. Can I get you some?"

"Yes, please. I think that would be good."

"Will you wait here for me?"

"Yes," she looked around, saw a row of chairs lined up against a wall, went over and sat down as quietly as a butterfly landing on milkweed.

I returned with two clear plastic cups of red wine. Fortunately, Adrianne's caterer friend had included some fairly decent kosher wines along with the traditional Concord grape varieties.

"Can you tell me about your husband?"

She crossed one leg over the other, hiking her skirt up further. I trained my eyes on hers so I wouldn't get distracted. Or give the wrong impression.

She took a sip of her wine, "He was an actuary."

"Insurance?"

"No. Actuaries work in any number of businesses. They analyze data and assess financial risk. Marvin had his own business. He consulted myriad clients," her grammar and vocabulary displayed an educated command of the language.

"And you?"

"Magazine editor. *Front Range Women.* A regional monthly, obviously focusing on women. Not that it matters."

There were any number of fellow writers' names I could have dropped that might cement a bond between us, but I didn't want to get off on a tangent. If there was any connection between Marvin Saines and Aaron Meckler, I wanted to know.

"Forgive me for asking," I said, "but why do you think your husband's passing wasn't suicide? And, that there may be a connection to Ms. Meckler's father? Did they know each other?"

She took another dram of wine, "Not that I know of, but you never know. They might have met. But that's not important. You asked about suicide. Very unlikely. Marvin had just surprised me with a European river cruise for our tenth anniversary. We were going to sail from Amsterdam to Budapest in June." I repressed my natural tendency to relate my relationship to the Hungarian capital. "One of the reasons we could afford the trip was because he landed a huge new client. A pharmaceutical company that's about to market a 'fat pill.' Everything was going our way. I mean, between us we were making a comfortable living. But the additional cash flow Prefaxal was providing, meant doing things we always talked about, like traveling and . . .," she looked down into her lap again and choked out something indistinguishable.

"I'm sorry Ms. Brown. I didn't catch that."

She raised her head, tears overflowed her eyelids. She dabbed her eyes with the cocktail napkin that came with the wine, took another sip, looked up at the ceiling to stop the tears, looked at me and said, "Doing things like traveling and, having kids. Marvin really wanted to start a family." She pressed the napkin to her face again.

She certainly had me convinced. I reached out awkwardly, and gently put my hand on top of hers. It seemed to help. I said nothing. She sobbed in silence for a few more moments, then looked at me again, "I'm sorry."

"No need to apologize. Take your time. Talk when you feel like it."

She sniffled, drank some more wine, gave her head a little shake and said, "Anyway, you don't hear much if anything about people hanging themselves. At least not with the traditional hangman's noose. That's so western. Belts, sheets, lamp cord; yes, if that's the way they want to check out. But not rope. Too trite. Besides," she continued in what seemed like a literary lecture, but which kept her from too much emotion, "Marvin couldn't even do a half-Windsor, much less a perfect noose."

"I see your point. What did the police have to say when

you shared your thoughts?"

She gave me a quick, sardonic smile. "They told me that he could have bought a rope from a western outfitting store and had them tie it, or gotten someone else to do it with some kind of story. They also pointed out that there was no sign of a struggle. And, he had taken off his glasses and set them aside, as, apparently, every suicide victim does. It seemed like they wanted this to be a nice neat package. No muss, no fuss, no overtime."

"When was this?"

"Three weeks ago. I buried Marvin two days later. He wasn't as prominent as the judge, so it was just two graphs opposite the obituary page."

"And now you want to compare notes with Ms. Meckler? Or join forces and pressure the police into reopening your husband's case?"

"Yes. I thought together, we might be able to exert some pressure. First just low-key, then go to the media if it came to that."

"Sounds like a good plan. But, can you put it off for a little while?"

"Why? How long?"

"Because Adrianne, Ms. Meckler, is still presiding over her father's memorial. And, because she's an artist whose one-woman show opens Friday at the gallery she owns in partnership with her late father."

She stared at me as if she were trying to piece together a jigsaw puzzle, then said, "You're a very compassionate man, Mr. Wren."

"Please, call me Sebastian."

"Elizabeth."

"I promise to look into your husband's and Aaron Meckler's deaths more thoroughly."

"You have credentials? You're with the police?"

"I'm not with the police, I'm a freelance journalist. I've

done a little investigative reporting, and I think I may have a small lead. Does the name Percy Claude Chaffee sound familiar?"

"No."

"What about PC Chaffee?"

"No. Why? Who is he?"

At that moment, Adrianne Meckler came from the reception hall. "Oh, there you are. Should have known you'd find a pretty lady to talk to while I shake hands, give hugs and thank about a thousand people."

"Sorry, Adrianne. This is Elizabeth Brown. She met your father a few years ago," I lied, "and wanted to pay her respects."

Adrianne noticed the balled up cocktail napkin and realized Elizabeth Brown had been crying. "I'm sorry, Ms. Brown. Thank you for coming. I really do appreciate it. If you and Sebastian will excuse me, I've really gotta pee." She didn't wait for us to reply, but bee-lined it to the ladies room.

"I better get out of here before she asks me about meeting her father," the astute Elizabeth Brown said. "Please call me, I really need to talk," she reached into her purse and pulled out her card.

"I'll be in touch, I promise."

***

All the guests for her father's memorial had finally left, when Adrianne asked, "Who was that woman again?" It was just after three and we were heading back to my place so I could change, then back to the AM Gallery so she could change. We figured everything would be all right at the gallery as the police would have called Adrianne or me if there was a problem. We could have depended on Horse to watch over the gallery, but he had been at the memorial with his wife and daughter, though they left over an hour ago.

"Her name is Elizabeth Brown," I didn't volunteer

87

anything further as I anticipated her next question, and was trying to concoct a plausible answer that would stay with the facts that I knew, and embellish as little as possible.

"And how did she know my father?"

"I'm not real clear on that," answering the question I figured she would ask. "Something about her husband, an actuary, who was doing work for a pharmaceutical company."

"What's his name? Why wasn't he with her?"

"He passed away a few weeks ago," I ignored her query about Elizabeth's late husband's name as I didn't remember it and, should she and Elizabeth meet, I wanted to minimize how many lies I'd be responsible for.

"What was the name of the drug company?"

"She was pretty broken up. Something like Prescott Pharmaceuticals."

She laughed. "Can't be Prescott, Sebastian. That's from the old *Colbert Report*." It was good to hear her laugh.

"Anyway, I was wondering if Aaron ever did work for a big drug company as an attorney, or maybe presided over a case involving one when he was a judge?"

"Not that he mentioned. But, attorney-client privilege, if not just ethical jurisprudence, would keep him from discussing his cases. And nothing he did on the bench was noteworthy enough to make headlines."

"That doesn't preclude him making a ruling that really pissed off some corporation. I'll get the name of the company and do some research."

The stop at my townhome was perfunctory. Adrianne lavished affection on Motley while I hung up my funeral togs and slipped into jeans and a shirt.

Although we could clearly see that nothing was amiss at her place, we double-checked the locks and gingerly swiped a finger across one of the newly painted, display walls, as if 20 hours might not be enough time for paint to dry.

Upstairs in her studio and apartment, everything was in order. "Turn around, please," she instructed me with unnecessary modesty. I did as I was told. A few moments later she came over to me in black tights, a beautiful floral print blouse that covered her equally-attractive butt, and a pair of pumps adorned with a classic Miro. "Thank you for today," she said, and kissed me on the lips with affection, but not passion. Her arms were up on my shoulders with hands clasped together behind my head, she continued. "Thank you for everything. You're a very fine man, Sebastian Wren. May I buy you dinner?"

"You don't have to do that."

"Precisely. But first, I want to go through these paintings again to see if I still want them to go where I thought they should go yesterday."

I had the distinct feeling she would change the arrangement another dozen times between now and her Friday opening. Since I didn't mind tip-toeing through her work again, I smiled my consent but was curious about one small item: "When you say these paintings, you mean your paintings?"

"You didn't like my father's starscape?"

It seemed like a loaded question. I was an idiot to ask. What the hell was I thinking? I blushed and was trying to think of a way to weasel my way out of it. She watched as I averted my eyes and looked about the room for something to comment on, to change the damn subject.

Finally, she decided to let me off the hook, "Dad could fuck up a paint-by-numbers canvas," she laughed. "However, that said, I don't care what anyone says, I'm going to hang that little picture on the wall in back. It will have a printed sign like all the other works. Only this one will simply say: 'Aaron Meckler,' his birth year and this year. And it will have a tag that says, 'Not for Sale.'"

Chapter 15

Dinner was a pleasant affair at a little bistro on Larimer Street. Once Denver's skid row, the block-long collection of chic shops and restaurants had been rescued from degradation by Dana Crawford in the 1970s. The dynamic woman went on to help create the trendy LoDo area, eventually involving many others, including a former geologist turned micro-brewer and restaurateur, who went on to become Denver's mayor, and then the governor of Colorado.

There was no need to try to impress Adrianne with my knowledge of recent history, facts I was sure she already knew. We talked of the warmth and prodigious attendance of her father's memorial and her plans for the gallery opening. As I suspected, she was already rearranging her paintings, but not her father's artwork.

The long day and a good bottle of wine left us both drained. We retired to our individual rooms. I was catching up on emails in bed when I heard some sniffling from the guest room. Before I could make up my mind whether I should go to Adrianne to comfort her, or stay where I was, I heard soft foot steps from across the hall. Then, "Go to your papa." And then I heard the click of the latch as she gently pulled the door shut. A moment or two later, Motley jumped up on my bed.

As the cat found his place among the crumpled covers, I

heard what could only have been a torrent of tears from the guest room. Then quiet. I never saw her cry or stifle a sniffle after that.

***

Monday morning could not have come soon enough. But that old proverb reminded me, "Be careful what you wish for."

"I guess it's not that unusual for professionals to meet." Adrianne said between bites of bagel, apropos of nothing.

"What?" I asked.

"That woman you were talking to in the hallway at the temple yesterday. It's entirely feasible that an actuary would come into contact with an attorney, or a judge. It's just unusual that they would be close enough for his widow to come to Dad's memorial."

"Yeah, that is a little weird," I said, figuring it better to agree with Adrianne than try to sell some idiotic rationale for why Elizabeth Brown had been there. Do you need my help this morning? I've got a few things I've been putting off that I should attend to," I broached the subject of going off on my own to find out more about PC Chaffee, and trying to change the subject at the same time.

"No problem. Horse is coming by to help put up my paintings. We haven't had any fires, break-ins or murders in the last few days, so I think I'll be all right. Especially with Horse there."

"Good. I'll drop you off and run my errands. I should be back at the gallery this afternoon, if you need me for some heavy lifting."

"Yeah. Couldn't do it without you," she teased.

"What about tonight? Would you like to stay here again?"

"If you'll have me. But let's kinda play it by ear, okay?"

"Sure."

I came into the gallery with her for a moment, just to look around. I was glad to see Horse was already there. He was sweeping up the sawdust and other detritus we'd left on the floor Saturday.

From the Santa Fe Arts District I swung west onto to Sixth Avenue and headed to the part of Lakewood I had printed out from Google and stashed in the case with my iPad. As I turned onto Sixth heading toward picture-perfect snow-capped mountains I pulled Elizabeth Brown's card from my pocket and spoke her number into the car's microphone.

"Elizabeth Brown," came the woman's voice through the car speakers.

"Ms. Brown, Sebastian Wren."

"Yes Mr. Wren. Thank you for calling. I was beginning to think I'd never hear from you."

"Sorry, Adrianne Meckler's been staying with me. I'm still concerned about upsetting her, so I waited to call. And, please call me Sebastian."

"That's very considerate, Sebastian. I understand, but I really need to talk with her. I'm sure there's a connection between her father's death and my husband's murder."

I let the allegation of murder go. "I'm doing a little investigating on my own this morning. How about we meet for lunch and talk some more. Then maybe the three of us can get together this evening?"

"Investigating? Using your superb journalistic talents?"

I let the sarcasm go, "So, I've been googled?"

"Of course. Nice work. Though nothing my magazine would ever want."

"Got it. What about lunch?"

"There's a micro-brewery with good food a block or two from my office; 16th and Curtis."

"Rock Bottom. Noon?"

"Make it 11:30 so we don't have to wait."

"See you then."

I clicked off and called John J. Hunt, administrator at the Englewood prison. I met Hunt a few years back when I contributed to an article for a national magazine. I was one of seven writers hired to do research for a feature writer at *NewsTalk*. One of those folks whose names appear at the very end of the article in mouse type that says, "Written by, name of staff writer, with, several other names, one of which would be Sebastian Wren."

Anyway, among us, we interviewed over 100 wardens or administrators. The article was not very complimentary to the overall system, especially facilities that had been privatized. But Englewood stood out as an exception. And, although we had nothing political, philosophical, ideological or compassionable in common, I thought that Hunt might remember me and give me a few moments of his time. I lucked out. After a quick reminder about the article, he did remember me, and he didn't hang up. Better still, he agreed to see me the next day.

The neighborhood where PC Chaffee was staying is another example of the diversity of Denver metro. Most of the small bungalows were quite charming, in an anachronistic way, considering it is the 21st Century.

I found the address I was looking for. A cedar-shingle-sided home of about 1,700 square feet on about three-quarters of an acre. I went up to the front door and knocked. I could hear the television inside. A girl of about eight answered. Her light blonde hair hung down past her shoulders. She was barefoot, wearing blue flannel pajamas. A woman's voice called out from another room, "Ella, don't answer the door, I'll get it."

"There's a man here," the little girl called back. Then to me, "I'm sick, so I didn't go to school today."

The woman came into view drying her hands on a dish towel. Judging by her hair and features, she was the little girl's mother. "Ella, you shouldn't open the door to strangers." Then to me, "Yes, can I help you?" She was sizing me up as she spoke and making sure she knew exactly where Ella was. She was tensed up as though calculating how to grab the child and run for it, in case of trouble.

What a shame, I thought, people have had so much fear drilled into them by talk TV and extremist media that they immediately assumed the worst in most any situation.

"I'm looking for Mr. Chaffee," I tried to sound as unthreatening as possible. "Mr. Percy Chaffee."

"You mean PC?" she seemed to relax a little.

"Yes, PC. I understand he lives here?"

"He's renting a room from us. Actually, it's just a little trailer out back. But it's hooked up to the septic and there's water and electricity." I wasn't sure if she was defending the dwelling or trying to rent it to me.

"Do you know if he's home?"

"Can't tell for sure. He's pretty quiet. Comes and goes. Minds his own business. You can just go 'round there," she swung the dish towel to her right. "There's only the one trailer."

"Thanks."

"If he's not there," she began to ask, "Can I tell him who's looking after him?"

"My name's," awkward pause, "Greeley, Horace Greeley, I'm a reporter. I'm just doing a story on," another awkward pause, "On inner-city rural living." Dumb Sebastian. Dumb. I could only hope she wasn't up on her literary or western history.

"Greeley. Like up where they raise all the turkeys. Wasn't that named for someone?"

Damn. Maybe she didn't remember the name Horace. "Yes. Like that, but no relation," I backed away from the front door as fast I could.

As soon as I rounded the back corner of the house, the trailer and an out building that probably had horse stalls, came into view. I knocked on the trailer's door and waited. After a few moments I knocked again, louder. Still no answer. I went around the other side of the trailer, more out of reflex than any particular reasoning. After circumnavigating the small silvery travel dwelling, I went over to the out building. A very large door attested to it being for horses. The building was only big enough for a couple of horses, tack and probably some hay.

The door was ajar, I easily slipped in sideways. No whinnies, so I assumed no horses. My eyes needed to adjust to the darkness. Strange sweet smell. I bumped into something. I nearly lost my footing. My vision cleared. I realized what I had bumped into. It was the black-clad body of a man dangling by a rope strung up on a wood cross beam. He had very blond hair. I nearly lost my breakfast.

Ignorantly and instinctively, I tried to help the man. With one arm about his hips, I tried to lift the dead weight as I reached up with my other hand to loosen the rope. Then pain seared across both my calf muscles and I went down. My head hitting hard-packed earth. Then darkness.

Chapter 16

My head felt like it was wedged between the spindles of an iron railing; my hands like they were entombed in cold, dry cement. Slowly, I opened my eyes. I saw shoes near my head on a dirt floor. Sturdy, sensible, clunky shoes. A cop.

It was coming back to me. PC Chaffee. Trailer. Horse barn. Body hanging. Sebastian falling.

Shit. I was on the ground in a horse barn in Lakewood where I inadvertently bumped into a body hanging from the rafters by a rope. Then something like a Broncos lineman slammed into me below the knees.

Before I could piece anything else together, the cop shoes shuffled over to me. Blue, serge-covered legs came into view. Then a face. Too close to focus. Next, a voice. So close I smelled coffee breath. "I think he's coming 'round."

He grabbed my right arm with both hands and half-helped, half-jerked me to my feet. I felt the iron bars tighten about my head. My right arm should have come free, but it was tethered above the hand to my left wrist. The motion added a stabbing pain to my left shoulder and the insulting realization that I was handcuffed.

My vision was blurry, but sharp enough to know there was no body hanging in the barn. There was the oaf who man-handled me to my feet. There was another man in slacks and a jacket. A third man in a white lab coat. And several other police-clad people milling about officiously.

There was also someone supine on the dirt floor—in a body bag. Next to the body was a rope. It had a greenish tinge to it. And a hangman's noose.

The man in the slacks came over to where blue-serge-oaf held me. "Sebastian Wren, I'm Lieutenant Gordier. Lakewood Police, homicide. Can you tell me what you're doing here?"

I clenched my teeth against the pain in my head, hands, shoulder and calves. My experience with the police was to try to be polite, despite the absurdity of the situation. And to answer questions directly. "I was looking for a man named Percy Claude Chaffee."

Gordier cast his eyes on the body bag—very subtle. "What business did you have with Chaffee?"

"Just wanted to talk with him."

"About?"

"About an attempted arson on Santa Fe a few nights ago."

"What makes you think he knew anything about your fire?"

"He matches the description of someone seen in the area at the time."

"How do you know? And, why didn't you call the police?"

Oops. Quick, writer guy, think of something, and make it credible. "A friend saw someone who looked like him. I asked around at the local bars, got a name, came here to talk to him."

"Yeah, sure."

"Why am I handcuffed?" I asked.

"Lady in front heard noises. We sent a patrol car, found your friend hanged. Dead. You on the floor. What do you think?"

And I thought I was having trouble with credibility. "I think I should have a lawyer."

"Oh, do you now?" the cop was loud, intimidating, doing

a pretty lousy James Cagney. But there were too many people around for him to really harass me.

I was on the verge of a snappy retort that would probably lead to more grief, when a familiar figure entered the barn.

"Lieutenant, I'm Detective Sergeant Rawlins, Denver PD. Captain Spooner suggested we might work together on this, since Chaffee was on our radar as a possible arson suspect. We were in the process of getting a warrant when we heard about the situation here."

Gordier didn't look pleased. Obviously, Spooner was the Lakewood Police Captain he answered to, which gave him no choice. "Well, since you were getting a warrant anyway. But I want to bring this guy in for questioning."

"I don't think you need to do that, Lieutenant Gordier. We can keep an eye on Mr. Wren. Besides, it isn't likely he's your man for this. In my 28 years on the force, 18 in homicide, I've never found a suspect passed out cold at the scene of a crime he committed."

"Well, it'll be on your head if you're wrong," Gordier grumbled back at her.

"I'll take my chances." She motioned for another officer to take the cuffs off me. One pain relieved, three to go; make that four, if you include my dignity.

Rawlins led the way. I followed, still limping from the impact of whatever bashed into my legs. At least I knew what happened to my head. The hard dirt, horse-shit-infused floor of a barn. I needed ibuprofen, lots of it. And a hot shower.

Rawlins slowed down a little when we were out of hearing range of the other cops so I could catch up. "What the hell were you thinking, Sebastian?"

"It didn't seem like DPD was doing enough to find out if Meckler was a suicide or a murder. By the way, thanks for getting me out of there."

"You're just lucky one of my guys heard what was going

on out here. Malcolm Gordier used to be with the DPD. He was a decent enough sergeant. Got lucky with a bust two years ago. Got cocky. Then he got 'retired.' Lakewood hired him 'cause he looked good on paper. But he's really just a gung-ho pain in the butt."

"The Peter Principal."

"What?"

"Never mind. How did he know who I am?"

"He looked in your wallet. What do you think?"

"I'm still muzzy. I would have thought of that."

"And, how did you know we were looking into Chaffee? No, don' tell me. It might hurt someone I'm very fond of."

Whew.

"Can you drive?" she asked as we approached a street cluttered with official vehicles. My Subaru and the neighborhood pick-ups and sedans stood out for their lack of blinking lights.

"Probably not the best idea at the moment."

"Give me your keys. The way you smell, I'm not going to let you ride in one of my cars. I'll have one of my people take you home in your car. Another officer will follow in a patrol car. You better get yourself checked out at a hospital. You got a blanket or something you can put over your seats?"

"Yeah, an old shower curtain in the back. And thanks. I really appreciate what you're doing."

"Don't mention it. I mean that. Don't you dare tell a soul."

***

It was one prescription-strength ibuprofen, a steaming hot bath, a mid-day snooze, and four hours later when I remembered I was supposed to meet Elizabeth Brown for lunch. My hands and wrists felt okay. My head and shoulder were down to a tolerable, chronic throb. I hadn't tried standing, so the jury was still out on the injury to my legs. But, there was no hope for my dignity. In fact, given that I botched the DPD's investigation of Chaffee, stood up the Widow Brown, and landed myself in a pile of horse shit, it would be some time before I felt good about my investigative abilities.

I rolled over to get my cell phone and call Elizabeth to apologize. It wasn't on the night stand where I always keep it. Oh yeah. It started to come back to me. One intelligent thing I did, was to have the cop pull the car into the garage. After he left, I lowered the door, took off all my outer garments, and left them in a heap on the garage floor—cell phone still tucked into the back pocket of my jeans, I hoped.

Gently moving my legs over the side of the bed, I found I could stand quite well, though not without pain. I twisted at the waist to look down and back. Purple and yellow bruises like dark plum bulls eyes tagged each calf. I slipped on jeans and a sweater and walked down the stairs as if they were made from a reclaimed bed of nails. In the garage I picked through the pockets of my jeans, removing my wallet, pocket knife, and cell phone. I turned the shirt inside out and bundled my jeans and socks inside to minimize exposing the messy, smelly parts to the house. I brought the bundle directly to the laundry room, dropped it into the washer and started the heavy duty cycle.

In the kitchen, I washed my hands as thoroughly as a surgeon, fixed a cup of tea and pulled out my cell phone.

Three messages from Elizabeth Brown, descending from the gentle trickle of concern into a tsunami of outrage.

Three messages from Adrianne going from the curiosity and exultation of "What time will you be coming by? I've got some incredibly good news," to the anxiety and concern of "Sebastian, are you all right? Please call me."

And, one message from Charles Love covertly telling me DPD found the body of PC Chaffee, his voice laced with a plea that I remain mum on the subject.

All three were of equal importance. I was wishing I had

two clones of myself so I could respond to them all at the same time. My aching body helped me prioritize. "Charles," I said when my friend answered his personal, private number, "thanks for your message. I think everything's okay, but I got pretty banged up. You working from home?"

"Yeah. What's wrong? Can we help."

"If you can get away, I need a ride to the ER I'll fill you in on the way."

"Sure thing. Give me a minute to wrap up here."

"Do what you gotta do. I have to return two more calls."

"You sure?"

"Yeah."

"Okay, just a couple of minutes then."

My next call was to Adrianne. Not that she was a higher priority, just that I thought I could make it a shorter call. I told her I was doing some checking up on a lead, got scraped up and that Charles would be by in a few minutes to take me to the doctor. I assured her that I was okay and that I'd catch her up on everything later. We had both totally forgotten to bring up her "incredibly good news."

My last call was Elizabeth Brown. I understood that she thought I was shining her on. This would take longer and needed more finesse.

"I don't want to hear any of your excuses, Sebastian," came the whirlwind of piercing accusations that followed my initial "Hello."

"I waited alone in that goddamn restaurant like an idiot for an hour. If you didn't want to meet with me, you shouldn't have even called. You need to have more respect for people. As soon as I get off work, I'm going over to talk to Meckler. Woman to woman. Then we're going to the police. So you can just go fuck yourself."

Knowing she was about to hang up I raised my voice and pleaded, "Wait. Wait. Please. Just give me one minute."

Her voice softened a smidgeon, but her tone was still

sharp as cactus needles. "What could you possibly have to say?"

"First, I'm terribly sorry," she started to fire another verbal shot through the phone, but I cut her off, "*And* . . . And, I need to get to the ER."

"What? Why're you going to the emergency room?" surprise replacing surliness.

"I was following up a lead for the arson attempt on Adrianne's gallery . . ."

"Arson? What does that have to do with my husband's murder?"

"Everything and nothing. All I know is that someone tried to toss a Molotov cocktail into the gallery she owns, owned, with her father. Anyway, when I got to his place, I found him hanging in a horse barn."

"Who? The arsonist?"

"Yes."

"Hanging? What? You mean like Marvin and your friend's father?"

"I'm not sure if there's a connection, or what it might be. I don't have a forensics team. I'm not a cop or a detective. So I've no way to compare the events."

"I know, but . . ."

"Please, Elizabeth. Don't get carried away with this. And please, let me get to the point. My friend will be here any minute to get me to the ER."

"Sorry. What happened?" caring replacing surprise in her voice.

"Something whacked me on my legs and I went down. Out cold. When I came to, there were cops everywhere."

"What did they tell you? What did they do?"

"They were about to arrest me."

"What?" it whistled out of the phone like hot steam.

"Exactly my sentiments. Listen, my friend Charles just walked in. Please, don't do anything rash. Can you wait until you hear from me?"

"Yeah. Sure."

"Thank you. I'll call as soon as I'm out of the hospital. Promise."

Chapter 17

Charles had me in the car and heading off to Denver Medical before he asked, "What happened? You don't look so bad, but you move like you're 90."

"I went over to Chaffee's this morning . . ."

"You were there? There's no mention of you in the report."

"You've got a good friend on the force."

"You mean Frankie Rawlins?"

"Yeah. Some cretin named Gordier from Lakewood wanted to bring me in. She convinced him not to. She also asked me how I knew about Chaffee, but then told me not to say."

"Gotta find a way to thank that lady. So, what happened?"

I told him the little I knew. Went over to Chaffee's. Checked the horse barn. Saw someone hanging from a rafter. Something or someone hit me low on the calves, and I went down like flaccid vermicelli. I woke up staring at cop shoes, a body and some kind of gas cylinder. I told him about Elizabeth Brown and her actuary husband, Marvin. But, neither of us could figure out any possible connection.

"Here's a little more I can tell you about your adventures this morning," Charles said. "I did some snooping when Chaffee's named came up on my computer. You know, since I told you about him, I set up an automatic alert on my laptop. Anyway, the lady in the front, her name's Hattie Moore, she said that after a suspicious man named Greeley came to her door this morning . . ."

"That would be me."

"Really, Sebastian? You couldn't do better than that? I hope you didn't tell her your first name is Horace."

Correctly reading my silent embarrassment, Charles teased, "Man, you are off your game. It's all these women, isn't it? So, Mr. Horace Greeley, your new friend Hattie Moore went over to her kitchen window and watched you walk around the trailer out back, then go into the barn. A few moments later, another man ran out of the barn and down the side of her house and jumped into a fancy new car across the street. He couldn't have been more than a block away by the time she called 911. The cops were there inside five minutes.

"She said the whole street filled up with police cars, ambulances, the works. Then she saw Greeley, that would be you, leave with a tall black woman, that would be Frankie, who escorted you to a police car. She figured you had just gotten arrested."

"So, now you know as much as I do. Which is damn little," I said.

"I got a little more. Rawlins' report indicates there's reason to believe that Chaffee and Meckler's deaths might be linked. The nooses were similarly tied. And, most importantly, Chaffee left a suicide note saying he was a member of a gang in prison that wanted to kill the Jew Judge for all the members he sent away."

"If you're trying to tell me that that wraps up Meckler's case, you're not being very convincing."

"Probably because I'm not very convinced. What convict with no known computer skills prints a suicide note on what forensics says is a very expensive HP color laser printer? And then doesn't sign it?

"Also, who else was in the horse barn? That man Hattie Moore saw running down her driveway and jumping into a luxury sedan? And, what was a cylinder of chloroform doing in the horse barn? Did the other man bring it along to knock Chaffee out? Or was it just to cripple you while he made his getaway?"

"Chloroform? What the hell is chloroform doing in a barn?"

"Not a clue. But I'm not a veterinarian, hell, I'm not even a cowboy. And that last part, I'm just guessing. Since the police didn't mention you being there, there's nothing about what hit you. But you said there was a cylinder of gas next to you when you came to, so I'm just projecting . . ."

"Good guess, if you ask me. Just drop me here. I'll check into the ER and get started. Did you bring a coloring book to keep you busy?"

"Yeah, sure. Got it covered." By which he meant his laptop on the back seat: the one that is always state-of-the-art with the latest security protocols and encryption. I was hoping he would dig a little deeper into what happened to "Horace Greeley" and his friends, while I got poked, prodded and x-rayed.

***

Fortunately, there were no fractures or concussion. I only had three bruises, left calf, right calf, fragile ego. All three would heal with time.

I gave Charles the good news when we were back in his BMW and heading for home.

"I wish I had good news for you."

"What did you find out?" I asked.

"Everything about this mess seems bogus. Either there is no link between Meckler's, Chaffee's and Saines' hangings—in other words just a big fat coincidence—or the whole thing is bull. I'm no fan of conspiracies, but this just doesn't compute."

"I was thinking in the CAT scan that it's time to get both women together and start comparing notes. There's gotta be a connection here somewhere. I'm no expert, but statistically, I don't think hanging, you know, traditional rope and hangman's noose—without a note—is how suicides go down these day. And, three in the course of several weeks? That's the definition of incredible. Also, it might be feasible that Chaffee had a hard-on for judge Meckler, but what about Saines? Or is that just some loose end we'll never know about? Would you mind sitting in on this? I'd love to have your professional opinion. Terri, too, if she's willing. She'll give it a different perspective."

"Thanks. I was hoping you'd ask. I'll give Terri a call, she can order in some pizza."

"Did Italian the other day."

"Chinese?"

"Such a cliché. Let's do it."

***

As Charles pointed his BMW up Speer Avenue toward our homes in Highlands, he called Terri and asked her to put together Chinese takeout for five and have it delivered to my place around six. After he clicked off the bluetooth, I hit redial on my phone to call Elizabeth.

"Seems like I'll live," I told her when she asked about the hospital. "Nothing broken, just banged up. Can you come over to my place after work this evening? I'll get Adrianne to come over and we can chat over Chinese with an ex-cop friend and his wife. Maybe we can figure out if there's any connection between Marvin's and Aaron's deaths."

"Did you find out something new this morning?" she asked.

"Oh yeah, I thought I mentioned it earlier. I was still

107

pretty muzzy."

"Muzzy?"

"Never mind. What I literally bumped into this morning was a man named Percy Claude Chaffee. He was hanging from the rafter of a horse barn in Lakewood."

"What the . . .?"

"Fill you in later. Can you make it?"

"Might be a little past six. I've got to swing by the house to walk and feed my dogs."

"If it's a problem . . ."

"No, they'll be fine. I'll get there as soon as I can. And get me some chopsticks."

"Sure," I said, wondering where that came from. Probably just a nervous reflex. I gave her the address, "See you in a couple of hours."

I clicked off and then pressed redial for Adrianne. I extended the same invitation and gave her a brief explanation of Elizabeth Brown.

"So you were holding something back from me. Do you think I'm some little wallflower?" I found her anger puzzling, if not misplaced.

"Adrianne. I'm sorry. That's not how I think of you. It's just that you have so much on your mind, and I wasn't sure who Elizabeth Brown is, or what I might find in Lakewood. I didn't want to get your hopes up or possibly upset you."

"I'd appreciate it if you'd let me make my own decisions."

"I promise . . ."

"What else haven't you told me?"

"On the way out to Lakewood, I called the chief administrator at the prison in Englewood."

"You know him?"

"Did an article a couple of years ago on prisons. You know, overcrowding, corporate-owned versus state-run."

"And you made him look good so now you have a contact?"

"Don't jump to conclusions. Out of 14 wardens or administrators who would talk to me then, John J. Hunt is the only one who I thought would take my call now. They've got a pretty good program out there. Of course, with inmates like the former governor of Illinois . . ."

"Don't digress."

"Sorry, thought you might see it as a stroke of luck. Anyway, I'm going to see him tomorrow morning. He was a great supporter of your father's mentoring. He said he would help anyway he can."

"And you thought I couldn't handle that?"

"Mea culpa. What about tonight? My place; sixish; Chinese takeout; Charles, Terri, you, me and Elizabeth Brown?"

"Make sure you get me some chopsticks," she replied.

What was it with the chopsticks? Whatever, if Terri doesn't get them included, I had plenty in a kitchen drawer.

Really, that's what they focused on, chopsticks?

Chapter 18

Adrianne Meckler was the last of the menagerie to arrive at what felt like a Hercule Poirot or Miss Marple gathering. Elizabeth Brown, the Loves and I were making small talk. Meckler was followed closely by a delightful spread of mostly Szechuan dishes, both spicy and mild; and enough chopsticks to go around. Terri Love and I spread boxes and bowls along my coffee table as Charles and Elizabeth sat down on the sofa; Adrianne folded her legs under her on a pillow on the floor. A bottle of red and a bottle of white also graced the table.

Although Marvin Saines' death preceded Aaron Meckler's by a few weeks, Adrianne kicked off the narrative, as far as it went. Charles chimed in with salient questions, while Elizabeth, Terri and I listened and observed, reserving our comments for later.

Charles took over when Adrianne finished, filling the others in about Chaffee. The most noteworthy aspects of his death were the inclusion of a note—not evident in Aaron Meckler's or Marvin Saines' suspicious "suicides," the chloroform canister in the horse barn, and his stay at the prison where Aaron Meckler mentored. Circumstantially thin, but very curious.

Elizabeth put down her chopsticks and began telling us about Marvin. "Outside of what insurance companies do to cover their corporate asses, I don't know much about actuaries," Adrianne said. "It doesn't sound very exciting. Forgive me, but maybe your husband felt like he was stuck in some really boring gig."

"That's a common misconception," Elizabeth answered evenly; one could tell she and her husband had been down this road before. "And, I'm sure that it would drive an artist up a wall. But he loved what he was doing. Yes, the bread and butter was helping corporations avoid risks that could cost them hundreds of thousands, if not millions, of dollars. But sometimes, by saving corporations tons of money, he was also saving people who would be affected by those risks from injury, even death."

"Hadn't thought of it that way," Adrianne said. "So, everything was going well? Forgive me for asking."

"No, that's perfectly all right. If we're going to find a link, we've got to ask the questions. And answer them honestly. Yes, everything was fine. Marvin landed a big contract late last year. It really increased cash flow for his business. In fact, we had thought that if they extended the contract, we might start a family."

"I'm so sorry about your loss," Terri said. "I know how the passing of a loved one can affect your entire life," she glanced my way, reminding me of what I went through when my wife, Heidi, died. "I hope you can press on and rebuild."

"I've got to. I know it's what Marvin wanted. We had discussed it, but we never really thought it would happen, at least not like this. Getting to the bottom of Marvin's death will help a lot, I think. Financially I'm okay. I'm doing well at *Front Range Women*, and Marvin's big client paid off their contract when they heard about his passing, which they didn't have to do."

"That *is* generous," Charles said, a hint of suspicion in his voice that only Terri and I heard. "What company?"

"Prefaxal Pharmaceuticals, they're ..."

"You said Prefaxal?" Adrianne cut in.

"Yes. Is that significant?"

"I don't know. It's just that . . . Sebastian, I told you I had some incredibly good news . . ."

"Yes?" I said.

"Well, it's just that this guy came by the gallery early this afternoon. He wanted to buy a couple of my paintings. I mean right then and there."

"Who is he? I didn't think you'd want to sell anything before the opening?"

"He's some *macher* from Prefaxal," she jumped up, got her purse off a dining room chair, and pulled out a card, "His name's Dwight Markham. He's some kind of executive there." She looked at the card. "Oh, he's the company president."

"Well, at least he's got good taste," I said.

"Not so much. He wanted Dad's painting, too."

Since no one else in the room knew what she meant, I said, "You know Adrianne's opening her one-woman show this Friday at AM Gallery?" They nodded as I looked at her and got a nod. "AM is both Adrianne Meckler and Aaron Meckler. They were partners. And, while her stuff is really good, at least I think so, she has a small painting her father did that's, well . . ."

"It sucks," she filled in. "But, it was my Dad's and well, I hung it near the office in the back. Ya know, just to honor him."

"We understand," Terri spoke for everyone in the room.

"But this idiot from Prefaxal said he really wanted it. He kept offering me more and more money for it. Even at $500 I told him it's not for sale. So he said if he couldn't have it, then he wouldn't take the others either."

"How many of your paintings did he want?" Charles asked.

"Two."

"How much were they?" Charles said.

"One is priced at $1,700, the other is $2,100."

"So you screwed yourself out of $3,800, I mean $4,300, over a painting you don't even think is very good?" Elizabeth asked.

"It's not about the money," Adrianne said. "I was going to put a 'Not For Sale' tag on it when I priced the other pieces. I don't care about the money. I'll sell those other paintings, I just can't sell that one."

"Of course not, I'm sorry," Elizabeth said. "I wouldn't be able to sell a pencil sketch my husband did, if he could sketch anything that wasn't on a spreadsheet."

"But the real issue here is, why was this Markham fellow so hot for your father's little painting?" I asked. "There's gotta be more to it than just complementing a couch in his office or something."

"And what's the connection with Prefaxal?" Charles asked

"Haven't a clue," Adrianne said.

Terri chimed in with, "They're an up-and-coming company that used to make generics of name brands. They're supposed to be coming out with a new fat pill. I heard about it from Marty Biegel, our broker. Apparently, the FDA is looking at fast-tracking its approval, but, because of some old rumors, they may be holding back."

"What rumors?" I asked.

"Marty said there's a rumor Prefaxal had been investigated for making inferior knock-off drugs to sell into third-world countries. Off the books, of course. But there never was an official investigation, much less any kind of prosecution."

"He wasn't recommending it?" Charles asked.

"Hell no, he was talking. Kinda Wall Street gossip."

"So what about this new wonder drug?" Adrianne asked.

"Marty said the preliminary studies show it to be very

effective and very safe," Terri answered.

"You know those early studies are funded and done by the drug companies themselves?" I said.

"Yeah, but if the FDA goes over the findings and approves it . . ." Charles said.

"Then Prefaxal's stock and sales go through the roof, just like Viagra," I finished.

"Even better. With the high obesity rate among both sexes . . .," Terri said with a look of keen interest. I didn't know if she was thinking of investing, or just buying the pills when they came out—not that she needed them.

"But how does that tie into the painting? What's this thing look like?" Elizabeth asked.

"Well, it's a starscape, I think," I said.

Adrianne reached into her purse and pulled out her cell phone. "Here, have a look." She passed her phone to Terri. She made a face then passed it to Charles. He raised both eyebrows as if he just saw a football player run into the wrong end zone. Charles handed the phone to me and I passed it along to Elizabeth. She looked like a person who'd been served calves brains.

"We get it," Charles understated. "So why?"

"Beats all hell out of me," I said. "I don't know jack about astronomy, but it doesn't look like any celestial panoramas I've ever seen. Adrianne, can you email a copy of that to Charles and me? Elizabeth?"

"Sure, what the hell. I haven't a clue how it can help, but you never know."

Adrianne got all three email addresses and the picture was immediately on its way to our various devices.

"What do we do now?" Adrianne asked.

"Maybe I can find out something about Chaffee's stay at the Englewood Prison. If he and your dad ever met there? Or if there's some other connection? But, I'm more troubled about this character from Prefaxal. Just doesn't fit in. Name's

Dwight Markham you said?"

"Yeah."

"I'll check on him, too. But I can't be involved in any of this, so Sebastian, you're gonna have to do the legwork. You know, since everyone else here has a real job."

"Piss off," I jibed back at him.

Chapter 19

The soft shuffle of footsteps approaching my front door caught my attention. Motley the fearless heard them too, and took refuge behind a stuffed chair. I was on my way to the door before the bell rang. It wasn't late, but pretty much anyone who might drop by unannounced was already here.

I saw Detective Sergeant Francine "Frankie" Rawlins through the sidelight and opened the door. "Good evening detective."

"Mr. Wren. I thought you and Ms. Meckler might be here. I hope I'm not imposing?" she looked past me into the living room. "Coffee klatch, cabal or conspiracy?"

"More coffee klatch than anything. We're just talking things out, trying to make sense of this mess," I spoke at a normal volume, then dropped to privacy mode, "we're hoping to give some solace to these women."

Rawlins nodded her understanding. "Perhaps I can help. May I come in?"

"Of course." She followed me into the house. "You probably know everyone, except for Elizabeth Brown, aka, Mrs. Marvin Saines."

The two women shook hands, Rawlins said, "A pleasure to meet you. I'm very sorry for your loss."

"You know about Marvin?"

"We had a briefing this afternoon. The DPD is looking into any recent suicides in the metro area that resemble the deaths of Meckler and Chaffee. So of course, your late husband's passing came up. Charles, Terri, always good to see you. Ms. Meckler, I hope you're doing all right."

"Hi Frankie," Charles said. "You want to join us? There's plenty of food."

"Didn't bring my chopsticks."

"Oh, there's plenty of those," I said.

"Not hungry, thanks."

"Why don't you sit down. Glass of wine?" I asked.

She looked at her watch. "Ten more minutes. Water for now. I'm off duty at eight. But pour me a glass for then."

"So what brings you by?" I asked as I provided both water and wine.

"I didn't realize you were all here. I just came by to let you and Ms. Meckler know that we're going to be digging deeper into Judge Meckler's death. And, that we're 99% certain your legs were hit with that canister of chloroform."

"Any idea what chloroform was doing in a horse barn in Lakewood?" Charles asked.

"Lieutenant Gordier said Chaffee had a sweet aroma about him when they took him down. According to the Jefferson County Coroner, chloroform can leave that kind of smell. But it doesn't linger in the body. So it wouldn't've been apparent on Meckler or Saines. I checked with our coroner and he concurred.

"Oh, so you think the man hanged in the barn with a suicide note was murdered, but not my husband?" Elizabeth said, her anger audible but restrained.

"Or, my father," Adrianne added just as curtly.

"I'm terribly sorry ladies," she said, looking at her watch and deciding, "what the hell," and lifted her wine glass.

"It's compounding evidence. That's why we're taking another long look at the deaths of your loved ones."

"About goddamn time," Elizabeth said in a poorly disguised stage whisper.

"I guess we deserve that. If I may go on?"

"Sure, whatever," Adrianne said.

Rawlins took another big sip of her wine and continued, "That leaves us thinking that someone knocked Chaffee out with the chloroform—the traditional way, not what they did to you, Mr. Wren—and then hanged him. Unlike the movies and TV, a chloroform knock out doesn't last very long. So Chaffee's murderer would have to keep the stuff flowing while he did his deed," she kept the description brief and undetailed for the sake of Adrianne and Elizabeth. "The good news for Chaffee, is that he was out cold and didn't feel anything," she said, which I figured was also for the sake of the two women.

"And, when you dusted for fingerprints?" Charles said.

"Charles, you know we can't discuss that outside the department. But, just between you and me, Chaffee's—either from handling it before his murder, or struggling to keep his killer from using it. There were also some partial smudges we're working on."

"Any idea how the chloroform got there?" Charles asked.

"I didn't think anyone used that stuff anymore," I said.

"Same thing I asked the coroners," she answered. "It's rarely, if ever, used as an anesthetic these days. There're much better and easier-to-control products now. However, it's still used worldwide in the production of pesticides."

"Who makes it in the US?" I asked.

"Several companies. Two are in Colorado. Delphinium Drugs has pretty much sown up business on the Western Slope. Prefaxal Pharmaceuticals services most of the Front Range and the eastern plains."

I don't know if Rawlins was aware of it, but there was a nanosecond in my living room where you could have heard Motley's whiskers twitch. A shock of realization went through the room riding on the back of the message, "Let's not say anything, gang." Realizing the deafening silence would give us away in another breath, I asked rhetorically, "What are drug companies doing in the pesticide business?"

"Are you kidding?" she said. "Deadly chemicals, big money. Check out logos on the jugs of bug killers and fertilizers the next time you're at a nursery or big box store. You've got big pharma right there alongside the petroleum companies. I guess you don't do much gardening, Mr. Wren?"

"Not my thing, hence the townhouse."

She took in my humble abode without comment. "Anyway, we're emailing both companies, and about a half dozen more in the nine-state region, to find out if any of their inventories have been compromised.

"Listen, I've gotta get home to my family. Thank you for the wine. Sorry if I upset you," she turned to Adrianne and Elizabeth. "Again, my condolences to you both. I'll let you know if anything develops."

I showed Rawlins out, closed the door and held my hand up to make sure she was out of earshot before breaking the silence, "I'll be go to hell."

"Why didn't we say anything about that guy from Prefaxal who wanted to buy Adrianne's paintings?" Elizabeth asked.

"Initially; just shock," I said. "But I'm glad we didn't. It just takes too long for the department to connect the dots and make a move."

"Here, here," Charles added. "But you know, it's not for lack of trying. There are rules."

"And," Adrianne said, "I'm sure it wasn't my paintings Markham wanted."

"I was thinking the same thing," I said. "Not that he shouldn't. But it really looks like he was only after your father's piece."

We all looked at the picture of Aaron Meckler's *piece de résistance* on our phones hoping for an epiphany. We may as well have been waiting for the second coming.

"There's gotta be something about Prefaxal on your husband's computer." I said to Elizabeth.

"I'm sure there was. But, the Prefaxal people were so nice about paying the balance on their contract, that, well, when they made it conditional on me allowing their IT team to erase everything on Marvin's computer that had to do with their business, I said, 'Okay.' They said he had proprietary information, and they wanted to make sure their competitors couldn't get it. It sounded reasonable to me at the time. And . . . well, the contract was worth thousands of dollars. I really screwed up, didn't I?"

"Don't beat yourself up," Terri came in compassionately. "It was a rough time. And I'm sure there was a lot of money involved. Besides, you had no way of knowing what they were up to."

"And," Charles followed up. "We don't know if the information they scrubbed might be relevant to your husband's death, much less Judge Meckler's and that creep Chaffee."

Elizabeth smiled gratefully at the couple. But she didn't look any more satisfied with Charles' supposition than the rest of us, including Charles himself.

"What about an external hard drive? Your husband must have had some kind of back up?" I said.

"Yes, he did. I used to tease him about being totally anal about that. He said there are only two kinds of computer owners: 'Those who have had a crash, and those who *will* have a crash.' But that's not going to help. He had a one-terabyte backup drive for everything. And then he had each client's files on separate flash drives, ranging from 16 to 64 gigabytes, depending on the individual need."

"What happened to all those backups?" I asked.

"Prefaxal knew about Marvin's backups. It's one of the things they said they liked about his business. Of course, they wanted to clean their information from the terabyte drive, and they asked me for their business' flash drive."

"Don't know if he realized it, but all that backup in the same place didn't cover him. You know, in case of a fire or a break-in or something," Charles said.

"What do you mean?" Elizabeth asked.

"I'm sorry. That was just a professional reflex. I didn't mean to criticize."

"No, no. That's all right. Please, tell me what you're talking about. At the magazine we have redundant servers in other parts of town. Just in case, as you said."

"Well, there are several companies that rent space on servers for off-site backup. They call them clouds, but it's just another set of computers somewhere with massive drives where subscribers can restore damaged or lost drives, upload data, apps, pictures, etc."

"What are the names of these companies?" Elizabeth pressed.

"Some of the best known are CampfireComp, iGeode, Bytesaver, Saferplaz . . ."

"The second one, iGeode."

"What about it?" I asked as the entire gathering inched closer to the edge of their seats—except for Adrianne, who was still on the floor, but leaned in like Seabiscuit at the starting gate.

"I turned on Marvin's computer the other day and there was a pop-up message from iGeode that read 'Your computer has not been backed up in 3 weeks.' I thought it was some kind of phishing, so I just clicked the little 'X' in the corner."

"Is the computer on now?" Charles asked excitedly.

"No. I just needed a phone number and I turned it off. Was that okay?"

"Not a problem," he said. "We can go over to your place, or his office, wherever it is. Do you know his passwords?"

"I can guess."

"Great, I'll be right back." Charles shot out of the house.

I got up and started to clear away dishes and the remaining food containers. Terri gave a hand while Adrianne got up on her knees to pour more wine. Elizabeth sank back into the couch, concentrating.

Charles was back before Adrianne had gotten around to all the glasses. Terri and I came back in from the kitchen. His laptop already open for business, Charles sat down and punched in the iGeode website.

"Okay, whatcha got?" he asked Elizabeth.

"His username was M_Bach. As in Marvin and his favorite classical composer. Like a lot of mathematicians, Marvin was a musician, too."

"And his password?"

She gave him five seemingly random letters, the pound sign and the number one.

"That's a really good password."

"The first five notes of his favorite Beatles song, which went to number one."

"I like this guy," Charles said, bringing a look of sadness to Elizabeth's face.

He pressed the enter key and waited a moment. "We're in."

Chapter 20

Charles scanned the files from Marvin Saines' computer. Adrianne Meckler, Elizabeth Brown, Terri Love and I maintained absolute silence, as if doing so would enable us to read Charles' thoughts, or see the computer images through his eyes.

Thankfully, Charles is a fast reader. "Okay. Thank goodness he didn't encrypt the individual files. It looks like Prefaxal had Marvin doing cost-risk analysis for a couple of different products the company produced. But I think most of them were just decoys, common prescription drugs that were already on the market, and whose benefits and side effects were already known.

"It appears that the main reason they hired him was to assess the efficacy of a new drug they're working on. It's called Plavynia ..."

"That's the fat pill Marty Biegel told me about," Terri said. "It's supposed to be safe and effective. The FDA is supposed to fast-track its release. It'll make billions for Prefaxal."

"That's interesting." Charles said. "What Saines was analyzing was a pill that effectively made people lose weight and, as long they take it, it will keep the weight off. However, as many as 10 in a 1,000 users will develop side effects like fatigue, excessive sweating and elevated body temperatures."

"That's one percent," I said. "So it would be 99 percent effective. Still pretty good, as long as people stopped taking it if they have the side effects."

"Not so fast, my friend. According to what I'm looking at, half of that one percent could die from taking the drug. And, it might cause irreparable damage for many others."

"So, Marvin's conclusions would certainly have made Prefaxal reconsider making the drug," Elizabeth said.

"Apparently not. If I understand all this, Prefaxal wanted to know how much it would cost the company to go ahead making and distributing the drug, versus how much they would earn, and how much liability they would suffer."

"But even with those numbers, they couldn't in good conscience go ahead with it, could they?" Terri asked.

"I think the key phrase there is, 'good conscience,'" I answered.

"Spoken like a true writer," Charles said. "Saines' numbers basically tell us that Prefaxal's first year's sale projections are $13 billion. Saines figured that 20,000 users would suffer some side effects resulting in 10,000 deaths. He then went on to interview top notch product liability defense lawyers, and concluded that of the 10,000 fatalities, they could persuade 93 percent of the families that the demise of their loved ones was due to other conditions, starting with obesity and then piling on high blood pressure, diabetes, and lifestyle habits such as smoking, drinking, being sedentary, etc.

"Of the remaining seven percent, that's 700 people, he figured the company would have to pay out about $35 million."

"There go their profits," Adrianne said.

"Drop in the bucket. Their profits, net of legal fees and settlements, are still in the billions."

"Would they do something like that?" Adrianne was incredulous.

"In a heartbeat. Pardon the pun," I said.

"But knowing that, how could the FDA allow it to happen?" Elizabeth asked.

"They wouldn't," Charles said. "So, Prefaxal must have found a way to make the drug safer. But none of that's here. Playing devil's advocate, and assuming they did find a way to mitigate the side effects, why would they want to erase Saines' hard drive? And, if this has something to do with his death, what's the connection? Sorry folks, I can't connect the dots. I don't see how Prefaxal could submit Plavynia to the FDA, as it was, and get it approved. They must have reformulated it, which makes this look like due diligence, not conspiracy."

Elizabeth and Adrianne were crestfallen. I was confused. Terri looked perplexed and Motley stretched and pushed up against my thigh.

"What'll we do now?" Elizabeth asked in a voice as soft as Motley's tummy.

"There's not much else you can do without some solid evidence. And it just isn't here," Charles said.

"Damn," Adrianne summed up everyone's mood.

"Wait a sec," I said. "There's still your father's painting. How the hell does that fit into this mess? Regardless of what Prefaxal was doing with their drug trials, there's still something there."

"Maybe we should go over to the gallery?" Adrianne said to me, hope bolstering her mood.

"Maybe that little painting shouldn't be left alone tonight," Charles said.

"I had an alarm put in," Adrianne said.

"That'll just slow a really good crook down."

"If you all will excuse us," I sprang up, looked at Adrianne, then said with a sideways glance, "Charles? Terri? Would you mind?"

"We'll pick up and lock up here," Terri said. "Just get

your ass over there before Adrianne gets another call from the police."

***

I went a little out of my way to cruise by the front of the studio, just to see if anything was amiss at the gallery. No one loitering outside. The door looked secure. A few soft lights inside gave potential passersby a preview of Adrianne's art. I hung a right at the corner and then swung into the alley behind the gallery. Everything looked fine. But just for a moment.

Another car swung in right behind me. Then a second car turned in at the far end of the alley. It only took an instant to realize that both cars had been waiting on the side streets, watching for either of our cars. There wasn't enough space to just accelerate and pass the car in front. It would have been even worse to throw my car into reverse and try to squeeze by the guy behind me. We were screwed.

In an instant, I thought to pull into a parking space behind a different building. "What're you doing?" Adrianne asked, as confused as a Baptist at a *bris*.

"We've been cut off front and back."

She twisted her head around and saw the car behind. Whipped her head back and saw the other car approaching faster than narrow alleyways allow. Not even a curse escaped her panicked being.

"Try and stay calm," I said. "Maybe we can convince them this is where we were headed."

"Good luck with that."

"Give it a try."

I boldly got out of my car and came around to the passenger door; not so much out of chivalry as to pry my petrified playmate from her seat.

"Don't even think about it, Wren," came a Thor-like voice reeking of stale tobacco. The man from the car behind was back lit by his headlights. In another moment a second apparition was silhouetted in the high beams of the car in front. I froze with my hand still holding the open car door.

I thought about all the heroes I'd seen on TV and in movies. From John Wayne to Bradley Cooper, and tried to imagine myself whirling about, smashing faces with fists and convenient nearby objects. Bullshit. I was scared. Not that I had a lot of experience with a situation like this, but these guys really knew what they were doing. No way to see their faces or the make and model of their cars, much less a license plate number. We were S.O.L.

"Let's just take a walk up the alley to your girlfriend's little shop," Tobacco Breath said, adding insult to injury. "Come on bitch, get out of the car."

Adrianne swung slowly out of the car, as if she had just been banged up in a multi-car accident. Indeed, she had been banged up good since her father's death. I was concerned about how much more she could endure.

"Let's go," the large man said, as he pushed me out of the way and pulled on her arm. She tried to jerk it back, but he tightened his grip.

She squirmed, and squealed, "Ouch." Then went limp from the waist up. Her head bobbed and her other arm swung loose. Even her legs just jerked along like Pinocchio on Zanax.

The other man fell in behind me and pushed me along. Neither had shown a weapon. I figured they had them. But that was irrelevant, their brute strength was enough to control an underweight writer and a petite woman with no combat training.

When we got to the back door of the gallery, Tobacco Breath told Adrianne to punch in the codes for the alarm and the door lock. She complied without resistance or reflection. We all entered the dimly lit gallery. Aaron Meckler's painting was hanging a few feet inside the gallery. Adrianne's chaperone simply reached in front of her and lifted it from its hook, turned his head toward the wall so I couldn't see his face, and left with his partner in crime.

It was like putting on a condom and ejaculating when you're about to get laid for the first time. Over in a flash. A feeling of complete failure and impotence. It took me a full, long, agonizing second to think of reaching for my phone. Another to dial 911. And, just as I was about to press Call, Adrianne put her hand on my arm to stop me. Her apparent numbness gone.

"It's okay, Sebastian. I'm tired. I'm tired of this whole insidious business, whatever it is. I don't want to spend the rest of the night explaining what happened to Detective Rawlins, or any other cop. Not even Charles. Let's just move the car, lock up and go to bed."

"But . . ."

"But nothing. It's okay."

I was about to protest again when it hit me. I smiled and said, "You're right, it's okay. I'll go get the car, lock the door behind me."

"I'll just close it and stay right here. Nothing else is going to happen. They got what they wanted. They won't be back."

A minute later I pulled my car into the space behind the gallery and let myself in. Adrianne was standing there as promised.

"Let's go upstairs."

She locked the door, took my hand and led me over to the bottom of the stairs. I let her ascend first. "Would you like some water, wine, or something stronger?" she asked. "I'm going to pour myself two fingers of Glenlivet."

"Make it two. You recovered pretty fast."

"What do you mean?" she said, getting two thistle-design, glasses from a cupboard.

"I thought you were going to collapse outside."

"My minor in college was acting. One of my favorite

songs from my father's era was Nina Simone's 'Go Limp.'"
She poured, handed me a glass.

"I know it well. Good thinking."

We were standing in front of the French doors, nursing
our Scotch and watching a late moon rising over the rooftops
of the city. It was bright and white, shining into her studio
and apartment, revealing the couch I had slept on, still
shrouded in the rumpled sheets and blanket that made up
my bed. I figured it would only take a few moments to tidy
it up for sleep.

"I'll call Charles in the morning and . . ."

"Shhh," she said, taking another sip of the single malt
whiskey. "Let it wait." She turned to me, "Will you sleep
with me tonight? I want us to make love."

I sipped my drink, simultaneously trying to emulate Errol
Flynn and decide if this was a good idea.

"I think I know what you're thinking. Is this attraction,
distraction or addiction talking?"

"Well . . ."

"Shhh. Don't question it. No strings, no commitment.
You're a man. That's supposed to be the ideal offer."

"I, uh . . ."

"Do you like movies?"

"Yes."

"Remember in *Zorba the Greek*: Zorba says something to
Basil along the lines of, 'There is one sin God will not
forgive. That's if a woman calls a man to bed and he refuses
her.'"

"Well, if it's God's will," I said, and turned to embrace
her, crystal whiskey glasses pressing into each other's backs.
Our free hands started to explore each other's bodies. I
quickly found her right breast and began to caress it. She
pressed her mouth even harder against mine and slipped her
left hand past my belt and down into my jeans.

Pulling back so slightly that I could feel her hot breath she said, "I think you've been ready for this for a while."

***

Two and four climaxes later, respectively, sitting up in her queen size bed with a light but warm duvet resting just above our waists, sipping a second round of Scotch, she asked, "How're you doing?"

"Very well, thank you."

"Yeah, I'm good, aren't I?" The question was rhetorical.

"And you?" protocol demanded I ask.

"Pretty damn fine, thank you."

"Besides getting laid, what're you thinking?"

"Same as you," her voice matter-of-fact, unhurried, unalarmed. "Those guys who were here, they're just hired dudes. Thugs or private eyes. Neither they, nor whoever hired them, understands the art business. If it's successful, it's like any other business. There's overhead, bookkeeping, insurance, cataloging and, especially, photographing inventory in case you ever have to file a claim. I shoot everything I produce or show in the gallery as soon as it's finished or logged in."

"Yeah. Got that. Besides, you emailed the picture of your father's painting to me and the group. If it's about the picture, we're good. If it was hiding something under the paint, or on the back, we might not be so lucky."

"Like a movie mystery? A treasure map? Maybe the magic formula for the fat pill? In your dreams." She reached down to her purse on the floor next to bed, moonlight reflecting on her nice round ass, and came back up with her phone. She opened her photo album and quickly made a few keystrokes. "There's an 11x17 printer downstairs. Tomorrow morning we can look more closely at the picture of my Dad's painting."

Despite the workout, sleep wasn't in the cards for me. I slipped quietly out of bed and walked about the room in bright moonlight. I didn't open any more drawers or look under placemats. Just peered out the windows, looked at her pictures, both painted and photos. I decided to go downstairs and look at the printout of the picture of Aaron Meckler's starscape.

I tiptoed to the door and eased myself down to the gallery. I figured the only place her big printer would be was in the storage area in back. My logic was rewarded with a perfect reproduction of the painting that was nearly the same size as the original.

I was studying the print under one of the soft lights in the middle of the gallery when soft footsteps approached. I knew it was Adrianne. She came up next to me wrapped in a robe.

"Sorry I woke you," I said.

"Had to get up to pee. Trouble sleeping?"

"Should be exhausted, but I feel energized. It's happened before."

"You mean I'm not your first?"

"I just couldn't stop thinking about your father's artwork."

"You're too kind."

"No. Really. It's got to be the key, or at least a critical part of the puzzle."

"I'm sure you're right. Why don't you bring it upstairs to look at. You know you're standing under a light in a gallery on Santa Fe Drive with large windows, and you're completely nude?"

Chapter 21

Never one to be overly modest, I just rolled up the print and ambled on up the stairs, only getting pinched twice by the vixen behind me.

We poured over the print for another half hour. Adrianne even pulled out a large magnifying glass. Nothing. Just the same old random pattern of shiny dots against a midnight-blue background. Most were white, some were blue. There were lesser amounts of red, green and yellow. Looked odd to both of us. But neither of us are astronomers. Not even amateurs.

"Do you think there's a constellation in all of this?" she asked.

"Beats hell out of me. I can find the Big Dipper. After that, I don't know jack."

"And the Dipper's not even in Dad's painting. Maybe it's another hemisphere?"

"Could be. I wouldn't know."

"Bed?"

"Yeah."

Sleep came easier after our midnight ramblings. Now I was exhausted. My late wife used to tell me that brain work can tire you out faster than physical exercise. I could definitely vouch for that.

The soft tone of a text alert awakened me as dawn gave way to a morning wrapped in a gossamer shawl, a rarity in

Denver. A fog like that usually burned off in an hour or two.

The message was from Charles: "Up 1/2 nite trying to ID M's stars on web. Got nothing. U home or @ A?"

I texted back, "A."

"Good?"

"Yeah, good."

"Today?"

"Prison a.m."

"Prison?"

"Englewood. Talk 2 M's mentorees."

"Talk later. We'll check Motley."

"Thx."

Adrianne was up on an elbow, "Charles, Rawlins or the widow Brown?"

"Charles. He tried to find the star cluster your father painted on the internet," I answered, trying to train my gaze on her brown eyes instead of her pert breasts.

"Any luck?"

"Nothing. Got anything for breakfast, or should we go out?"

"You're always thinking about food."

"Not always."

***

"Are you still going to see what's-his-name at the prison?" Adrianne asked me over coffee, bagel and a schmear in her kitchen.

"John J. Hunt."

"John J., huh? Sounds like a real ball buster."

"He is. Reminds me of my junior high school vice principal."

"So you're going?"

"Absolutely. Want to come along?"

"Not really. Probably better if it's just guy to guy. Besides, I still have a boatload of stuff to do here. And, I want to go by my father's place, if the police will let me in."

"Looking for anything in particular?"

"Hadn't even thought of that. Just felt like I should go over and make sure everything is okay. Maybe look around for some keepsakes, you know? But if I do find something, I'll give you a call, or text."

"Tonight?"

"Is it okay if we play it by ear? Last night was good for both of us. But I don't think we're into something long-term or committed just now."

Had to admit that I was relieved, "You've got a good head on your shoulders, Ms. Meckler."

"Just on my shoulders?"

I smiled, and got a little hard.

***

At the prison, they had me do everything except drop my trousers and spread my cheeks. When the search was done, I was escorted into Hunt's office. "Mr. Hunt. Thank you for making the time to see me," I said as we shook hands.

"Thank you for not lumping our prison in with those egregious bastards who think making a fat profit off tax payers is good business. Sorry to hear about Judge Meckler. He was really making a difference for some of our guys. How is it you knew him?"

I gave him the briefest explanation I could.

"So, how can I help you?" he asked.

"If it's possible, I'd like to talk with the men he mentored."

"I thought that might be the case from your call yesterday. Some of the better ones have already been paroled. I'll have my secretary get you a list of their most current addresses so you can track them down later, if you want.

"As for the men that're still here, I've arranged to have them meet with you in an interview room. There's only three, I'll have an officer bring them in one at a time."

"Thank you," I said. I appreciated that he always referred to the inmates as men, not perps or fish or cons. Gave them a little dignity, whether they deserved it or not.

The first man I interviewed was Geoffrey Wallace. He was serving 15 years for armed robbery. He held up a liquor store and left with just over $2,500 in cash, along with a stack of checks. "Meckler, he was an all right guy," Wallace told me. "He's the first one to hip me to the math. I couldn't do nothing with those checks, and forget about the credit card stuff, they're not even in the registers anymore. So, for the time I've got in here, minus the $200 I paid for the gun, I made out with a little more than $150 a year. Shit, I could make that in a couple a days just slinging fries at Mickey D's. Not fucking worth it. Meckler, he said I should find out what I'm good at. I'm pretty good with my hands. So, he got me into some classes here fixing stuff. If I do good and stay straight, I maybe can be outta here in six years, maybe get a job fixing appliances or something. Make a lot more money, and stay the hell outta this place."

"Can you tell me anything about an inmate named Chaffee? Percy Claude, or PC Chaffee?"

"I knew the dude. At least, like you know anyone in here. He was always in peoples' faces, ya know? Like one of them kids in school that's always pickin' on someone smaller."

"Yeah, I know the type. A bully. Did Meckler mentor him?"

"No. I think he met him once. But then Meckler said he had to, ah, excuse himself?"

"You mean, recuse himself?"

"Yeah, that's the word. On account that he was the judge what sent PC here."

"You said that Chaffee was a bully. Was there anyone in particular he pushed around a lot?"

"There was Doc. But Doc worked in the clinic, so Chaffee couldn't get at him too much."

"What's Doc's name? Did you call him that because he worked in the clinic? Like an EMT? Or a nurse, or something?"

"It's the other way 'round, from what I heard. He worked in the clinic because he was a doctor, a real doctor. His name's McIntosh. Don't know the first name. Everyone just called him Doc. We could have called him Doctor McIntosh. But Doc McIntosh sounds kinda funny. Ya don't wanna make fun of someone who's gonna be putting his finger up your butt. Anyway, yeah, he and the judge were real good friends."

"How do you mean? Did Meckler mentor him too?"

"Naw. He didn't need no mentoring. He's okay the way he is. I think they were friends because they were both real smart. You know, college and everything."

"You've given me a lot of information, thank you. That pretty much wraps things up, unless there's anything else you can tell me about Meckler, Chaffee or Doc?" I asked by way of ending the interview, but also putting the man at ease to reveal more; a technique I always employed doing interviews. Sometimes it paid off big time. People would relax and memories would get jogged from the relief of feeling they were off the record. On the other hand, sometimes it just meant that I'd gotten to the bottom of the well, and now it's dry. This was one of those times.

The next two interviews reminded me of taking pictures when I traveled. I usually got what I wanted with the first shot, the rest were just inferior copies of the original. However, the other two confirmed the friendship between Doc and the judge. I needed to add McIntosh to my interview list.

A guard took me back to Hunt's office.

"How'd it go?" he asked.

"Pretty good, I think. I'll know more when this mystery plays itself out. You know, Mr. Hunt, all three of Meckler's mentorees here mentioned Doc. Is there any way I can talk with him while I'm here?"

"I'll arrange it. It's getting close to lunch, would you like to join me?"

As much as my stomach was saying "Yes," I deferred. I really didn't care enough for this officious administrator to try to make small talk over prison fare. And I certainly wasn't going to discuss what I was trying to learn about the hangings. "I wish I could, but I've got another commitment in about an hour. I could use some water though."

"Sure thing," he said, picking up his desk phone and arranging for me to meet Doc in the clinic and to be provided with a bottle of water, since I wasn't allowed to bring my own in with me.

As I was being escorted down to the clinic, my cell phone buzzed. I pulled it out of my pocket and had a look. It was a text from Charles. I clicked it on. His message above a picture of a very polished-looking man read, "Thought this might come in handy. It's Markham."

I didn't bother to reply.

Chapter 22

The prison clinic was larger than I expected. Half a dozen beds with all the usual plug outlets, tubes, oxygen tanks, glass-fronted cabinets—locked, of course—privacy curtains, and all other accoutrements that depict modern medicine. It smelled of disinfectant. You could eat off any surface, including a floor that shined like a drill sergeant's boots.

Doc was Doctor Albert McIntosh. A short, wiry man in his late 60s. A full head of white hair in waves my great aunt Vera would have killed for. A ruddy red complexion revealed his Irish roots and his hair's certain red heritage.

At first, he picked a spot just below my shoulder on which to focus, so he wouldn't have to look me in the eye, or stare down at the floor like a scolded puppy. At first, I didn't understand.

"How can I help you, Mr. Wren?" he asked after introductions.

"It's Sebastian. And, may I call you Doc?"

"Sure. Everyone here does."

"What about before you came here?" I asked good naturedly. It was obvious I needed to get on a more friendly level before I could start to excavate whatever information or insight he might have stashed away.

My query was rewarded with a small smile, "Before I came here? I guess everyone called me Doc."

"What kind of medicine did you practice, Doc?"

"I never actually had a practice. I stayed at the university for a long time after graduating, doing research, assisting in labs and helping the teaching staff."

"You said you never actually had a practice. What do you mean?"

"Oh, well, I volunteered some at free clinics. And pretty much anytime a neighbor or family member needed a little attention, sometimes even their pets. But don't tell anyone, I'm not a certified veterinarian."

"Not to worry. Sounds like you had a rich and rewarding life and medical career."

"Thank you," he said, his sky blue eyes meeting mine for the first time.

"So, you have family?"

"Oh, yes. My wife Barbara. We were married for almost 40 years. She passed away five-and-a-half years ago." His eyes twinkled at the memory, and I was sure if I pressed, he would tell me the exact time down to the number of weeks and days.

"What about children?"

The twinkle left his eyes. "Three. Two daughters and a son."

"I'm sorry. They haven't passed, have they?"

"No. They're very much alive. But I'm not."

"How do you mean?"

"It's this prison business. They stood by during my trial. But after I was found guilty, they were ashamed. I can't say I blame them. What decent person wants a felon for a father? I haven't heard from any of them in over a year. No visits. No Christmas cards, or pictures of my grandchildren. I must be dead to them."

His own words cut him as deep and painful as a dull scalpel. But, at the same time, they were building a bridge that began to link us.

"Can I ask you what happened?"

"You mean you don't know?" he said.

"No. But I'd like to, if you don't mind." I didn't think Doc's incarceration had anything to do with Meckler's death, but I felt I needed to fully gain his trust. And there's no better way than to just listen. Besides, there's no such thing as too much knowledge or information.

"It's public record. But the short version is that after I retired from the university, a drug company hired me to consult on their research."

"What was the name of the company?" I asked, eager as a blue pointer to hear the name Prefaxal.

"Rexacin."

"Oh," you could almost hear me deflate as the air went out of my thesis.

"They made generic formulations of prescription drugs after the patents ran out. They were making millions. The work was easy. Basically, duplicate the original drug and add enough inert ingredients to effectively change the formula so they wouldn't get sued. The pay was good, but compared to the work we were doing at the university, well, it was almost shameful. I kept telling myself that I was helping to provide cheaper drugs for people who couldn't afford the hugely inflated prices of big pharma. And then, Rexacin stumbled onto a formula that can reduce weight."

I shifted my brain into high gear. This was sounding like Prefaxal. Who was screwing whom? I wondered. This can't be a coincidence.

"That would be worth a fortune," I said.

"Yes. If not for the fact that it would also kill or injure thousands of people."

"So, they didn't develop it?"

"We tried to reformulate it so it would be safe and effective."

"And you succeeded?"

"Nope. Can't be done. But, in their greed, they said they

wouldn't give up. They rationalized it by saying that if Rexacin didn't develop it, their competitors would."

I was beginning to see a pattern form, or was it a business plan? But how did Prefaxal, Meckler, Saines and Chaffee fit in with Rexacin? I leaned in.

"I told them I didn't care about their profits or their competition. I said that if anyone tried to bring it to market, I would reveal the formula and its results to the FDA, maybe even go public."

"What did they do?"

"Well, the next thing I knew, I was being arrested for corporate espionage. The police found the molecular diagram for the drug in a desk drawer in my home. The home my wife and I lived in the whole time we were married. Where we raised our kids. I could never have done that. I had been framed."

"Did you ever have that diagram?"

"Of course. But it never left the office. You're going to ask how it got into my desk drawer at home? I don't know. Anyone could have snuck into my house while I was at work, or with my children and grandchildren. It wasn't Fort Knox. There was nothing important or valuable there."

"I hate to ask, but, if you didn't sell the formula to Prefaxal, who did?"

"Prefaxal? Nobody had to sell anything to Prefaxal. Rexacin is Prefaxal."

"What?"

"In their lust to make more money, and after I was arrested. Rexacin started selling low quality prescription drug knockoffs into third world countries. And, some of them were repackaged and sold back into the US."

"And," I finished the narrative for him, "then they were bankrupted by lawsuits, lawyers' fees and court costs, and ultimately reorganized as Prefaxal."

"Now you're getting the picture," Doc said.

"So, you *were* framed," I continued. "But how does your friend Aaron Meckler fit into this mess?"

"You knew the judge?"

"Unfortunately, we never met. But I'm close with his daughter, Adrianne."

"It's a terrible thing that happened."

"It is."

"Suicide is the last thing I would have expected from the judge."

"Adrianne too. And, from what's been going on in Adrianne's life, it seems more and more unlikely."

"I never met her. The judge talked about her all the time. Please convey my condolences. I'm sure she's very upset. At least he's at peace and she can get on with her life."

"I'll tell her. She's doing pretty good, under the circumstances. She has a one-woman show this Friday at the gallery they owned together."

"This Friday? Already? The judge told me all about it. He was so looking forward to it. He said that, after all she had been through, it was like her coming-of-age. A second bat mitzvah. He wanted so much to be there to support her and her work. He was very proud of her."

"Precisely. That's one of several things that don't add up. Your confirmation of what Adrianne said, 'that he was looking forward to it,' that's not the profile of someone who is suicidal."

"I'm not a psychologist, but you're right about that. Did you say there were some other anomalies?"

"Yes. First, someone tried to break into their gallery. Then, someone tried to set it on fire. And finally, an executive from Prefaxal tried to buy some paintings before Adrianne's show would open," as I said the last, I reached for my phone and opened it to Markham's picture. "You may know this man?"

"Oh yes. He's the CEO of Rexacin. I mean Prefaxal. That's his headshot from the annual report. You get this off the internet?"

"A friend of mine did."

"It's not very accurate, it's at least 10 years old," he smirked at the man's vanity. "You know, he somehow convinced the district attorney that my 'heinous' crime deserved to be prosecuted to the absolute fullest extent of the law. Twenty years for having a piece of paper."

"That's harsh," I said.

"It's blood under the bridge," Doc said. "Is the judge's daughter all right? What about the gallery?"

"Everyone and everything is fine," I answered. "Any idea what would be the DA's motive for going along with Markham, if you're right?"

"Whatever suits the fancy of an ambitious public figure. Some private adoration from a hired fan, if you get my drift? Money. Maybe a stock tip that would pay off big time."

"Like a little drug company that makes generics bringing a pill to market that reduces weight without exercise or dieting?"

"Yeah, like that. So, the judge's daughter sold some paintings to Markham? Hope she made a bundle."

"She wouldn't sell them."

"Why not? Isn't that why painters put their work in galleries? To sell them? To make a bundle, and paint some more?"

"Well, yes. But Markham really only wanted to buy the one painting her father did."

"So, the bastards didn't get it?"

I didn't understand his concern over the judge's less-than-artistic dabblings. "Why do you think the painting is so important?" I said. "Besides, all I said is that Markham failed to buy it. But last night, some goons came by and stole it. They cornered Adrianne and me in the alley behind her studio. Then they forced her to open the door to the gallery, grabbed the painting, and left."

"Do you think Markham hired them?"

"It's the only explanation that makes sense."

"So, he has the only proof of the damage his company is about to unleash on the most vulnerable people in our society. And, the only proof that might clear me."

I was confused and frustrated about his agitation and just asked straight out: "What the hell is the significance of that painting? How can a bunch of stars that don't exist in the universe have anything to do with you, Prefaxal, Judge Meckler or anything? And, how can it clear you?"

My outburst slammed him like a gale-force wind. He looked back down at the floor. Immediately I knew I had over reacted. I was about to lose him. I had to reestablish our connection, our friendship.

"Doc, I'm so sorry. Just a few days ago, I didn't know either of the Mecklers, had never heard of Prefaxal or any of the other things we've been discussing," I kept rancor and frustration out of my voice. "I was working on a magazine article and got sucked into this whole affair. There are some really good people who have lost their lives over this. Others who are on the verge of ruin. And you. And, I have to say that I really like you all and want to help."

He looked back to see if my face and body language would confirm my words.

"Well, I have to admit," I continued, "I don't think I really give a tinkers damn about Chaffee and Markham. But I'm really beginning to like you."

At that he smiled, and began to explain. "When I was arrested for 'corporate espionage,' for stealing Rexacin's, Prefaxal's, formula for the fat pill, the company claimed I was going to sell it to a competitor. But, the key molecule in the formula that actually works to reduce fat, is represented by the judge's painting."

"Sorry, I'm not following you."

"The drawing the police found at my house is of that

molecule. Make a few changes to its structure, and you have a very safe drug. But it's only 15 percent as effective as the original for reducing fat. The original formula is 95% effective, but has major side effects. Markham and his board of directors sent data about the weight loss effectiveness of the drug to the FDA based on the use of the bad formula. But the data that touted the safety and negligible side effects of the drug were from the formula they submitted."

"Okay, just because we journalists like to make things clear on an eighth grade level: Formula A is very effective in reducing a person's weight, but can have dire side effects. Formula B is not very effective for losing weight, but has few, if any, side effects."

"Right."

"And, Markham and company sent the positive, weight loss, stats for formula A to the FDA along with the molecular structure of formula B, right?"

"Now you've got it."

"But wouldn't the FDA catch the discrepancy?"

"Not necessarily. They are tremendously under-funded and under-staffed. The two formulas are so similar, it's a good bet that it will slip through," he told me.

"Okay. So I understand how they're planning to defraud the public.

"And kill innocent people," he added.

"Of course. So, if we have a copy of the dangerous formula, we can get it to the FDA, they can compare it to the formula submitted by Markham and company, and not allow Prefaxal's fat pill to come to market."

"Exactly."

"And somehow, you convinced Judge Meckler of your story?"

"Gradually, over about six months. I tried to tell others before. But everyone thought I was just some senile, old, nut case. My first mistake was confronting Markham. Then, in my ignorance, I tried to convince the DA and prison officials. The more I talked, the worse it got. So I decided to just keep my mouth shut and wait. Work here in the clinic where I could do some good, and hope my contributions and good behavior will allow me to walk out of here while I still can, and not be carted out in a body bag.

"When the judge started his mentoring program, I went in for an interview. After I told him I was a doctor and had done research, he realized I wasn't there for mentoring, but for companionship. I didn't mean to mislead him. I sincerely wanted to spend time with another educated person."

"What about the chief administrator, John Hunt?"

"Too narrow-minded."

"Got that."

"At first, I kept the whole conspiracy-frame-up thing to myself, biding my time for the right moment to bring the judge into my confidence. But after a few visits, coffee, chess, talk of national and world affairs, I stopped thinking about my situation and just cherished our visits. It was actually the judge who started to ask me about my incarceration. By then, I was only too eager to share my plight with my new friend.

"It was his idea to look into the court records. As a former judge, it was easy for him to get my file. He had been looking at dozens of files in his capacity as a mentor. Of course, he wasn't allowed to take the files, or anything in them, out of the courthouse. They also don't allow cameras or cell phones into the file rooms. So he did his best to memorize the drawing of the molecule in the file."

"There was a copy of the deadly molecule in the file?" I was incredulous.

"Yes, the one that was planted in my home. It was evidence. The DA and Markham must have figured that once the case was closed, it would be as safe there as in the Prefaxal vault."

"Wow, that's hubris. Lucky for you the judge came along."

"In more ways than one," Doc continued. "Anyway, after the judge scrutinized and tried to memorize the diagram of the molecule, he drove over to the gallery, because it was closer than his home in Cherry Creek. He grabbed the first things he could to get the drawing down before he forgot it. And that was the acrylic paint and a small canvas his daughter had in the studio."

"Amazing memory," I said.

"Good, but not amazing. He went back and checked, then went back to the studio and made corrections. Then he took a picture with his phone and showed it to me. It looked like just a bunch of dots or stars or something. Not a molecule. But, when one connects the dots, literally, it becomes obvious that it's a molecule."

"So that's the significance of the different colored stars. You connect the reds to the reds, the whites to the whites, the blues to the blues, and so on," I said as if I had just stubbed my toe on the Rosetta Stone.

"You've seen it?"

"Better," I pulled out my phone and showed him the picture of Aaron's "starscape."

"Oh, my heavens. He made the final corrections," McIntosh whispered at the phone, then looked up at me, "I told him about a couple more corrections he needed to make to get it right. We never visited after that, I didn't know if he had time to make the changes before his death."

"Before he was murdered," I said.

Chapter 23

"If I understand you correctly, before you had a chance to take your information and that drawing of the molecule to the FDA, you were framed and silenced?" I asked Doc.

"Yep. That's the long and the short of it."

"And, because the case was over and done with, and nobody, not even your kids, wanted to pursue it, the drawing of the critical molecule was stuck away in a folder on a shelf in a warehouse full of papers, like the final scene in *Raiders of the Lost Ark*?"

"I'm sure it's not that dramatic."

"Yeah. Sorry."

"That's okay. If you can stop them and solve the judge's murder, you can make this whole damn thing as dramatic as you like. I just want to get the hell out of here and see my children and grandchildren."

"We'll sure try. But, how does the drawing exonerate you?"

"For one thing, my fingerprints won't be on it."

"What about the judge's fingerprints?"

"He brought along rubber gloves."

"Good. And . . .?" I asked.

"And, I have no need for whatever money they're saying I would have sold the formula for."

"Hard to prove a negative," I said. "And conventional wisdom says that everyone wants money. Unless you're a monk, or dead."

"Or dying, Mr. Wren."

"What?"

"Intracranial neoplasm. In my case, an inoperable brain tumor. Why would I risk prison and the alienation of my family for money? All I want is to be with them before I die."

"I'm so very sorry to hear that."

"I've had a good life. I miss my wife. I'm at peace with it."

"One might argue though, that you had nothing to lose, and that you wanted the money for experimental treatment. Or to leave a legacy for your family."

"I suppose so. But it's not the case. Thankfully, my children have done well for themselves and, I'd rather not be some doctor's or drug company's guinea pig."

I chose not to bring up the irony of his last statement.

"I hate to play devil's advocate, but is there any other possible reason the drawing could help clear you?"

"I'm a doctor, not a biochemist. I wouldn't express the formula as a picture of a molecule. All my other work shows that I do detailed, simplified reports. Not to the eighth grade level you may write to, but clearly and precisely. So it would be hard for any peer to misunderstand my hypothesis or conclusions."

"That's a bit thin, but maybe, with everything else, it will stand up. Is there anything else you can add?" I asked.

"No, Sebastian. Thank you for listening. I wish I was more confident that you can actually do something."

"I'm pretty sure you've given me all the key elements. With a little luck, and the help of some dedicated friends, I think we can help. Here's my card, I assume there's a way you can get in touch if you think of anything else?"

"Yes. I have some privileges. Thanks again."

***

It seemed to take glacial speed to get to the parking lot. Instead of calling Charles then and there, I got in my car

149

where I could talk and drive, though I was so excited, I wasn't sure where I was going to go first.

"Sebastian."

"Hey Charles."

"How'd it go?"

"Unbelievable. I think I've got it," I said, turning north on Kipling Street.

I related Doc's story.

"Was he one of the inmates the judge mentored?"

"No. I talked with three of the mentorees. All three mentioned Doc. That's Doctor Albert McIntosh. He and Judge Meckler just became friends because they were both professionals, you know, birds of a feather."

"So what's your next move?"

"I'm almost to Santa Fe. I think I'll go by the gallery. Adrianne has an 11x17 copy of the painting on the the printer she has there. Thought I'd bring it home and, as Doc advised, connect the dots, literally."

"What the hell does that mean?"

"On the printout of the painting."

"Oh," he said, but didn't sound convinced. "Mind if I come by and help? I'm hell at sharpening pencils and holding down rulers."

"Cute. I'll give you a call when I leave the gallery. Shouldn't be more than a half hour."

"Uh huh," he mumbled skeptically.

***

Of course, Charles was right. It would be an hour and a half before I left the gallery. Besides having to deliver a near-verbatim recount of my conversation with Doc—which elevated her mood with every revelation—she couldn't find the picture of her father's painting on her phone.

"I'm so technologically retarded," she said. "I must have screwed up and deleted it after I sent it to the printer last night. I'm so sorry Sebastian."

"Shouldn't be a problem. You've got an all-in-one printer, we can make a copy of the print from last night. Then we should keep one here, and Charles and I can play connect the dots with the other."

"Of course," she breathed a sigh of relief. "I would have thought of that—about two weeks after my opening. Could you take care of making a copy? I've got to get back with Horse to finish arranging the gallery."

"I was going to ask if you want to come with me?"

"I'd love to, but I've gotta stay here. I'm sure you and Charles can work it out. Probably even faster if I'm not there. What happens next?"

"I guess we'll take what we have to Sergeant Rawlins."

"I'll keep my fingers crossed," she leaned up and gave me a quick kiss goodbye.

I got the printout from her apartment, came back down, made a copy and took the original back upstairs. "Call me about tonight," I shouted to her as I left through the rear door.

As promised, I called Charles when I pulled out of the alley behind AM Gallery.

"You eaten lately?" he asked.

My stomach wanted to answer for me, but the phone couldn't pick up the muffled grumble. "No, and now that you mention it . . ."

"Terri thought as much. Come to our place, she's got some homemade chicken soup going."

***

Terri's chicken soup was always fabulous, but pushing my blood sugar decline to the limit, made it even better than the finest steak dinner; hunger makes the best sauce, as my late wife would say.

After lunch, Charles and I went over to my place. Motley greeted me with the mixed expressions of "Where the hell

151

have you been?" and "Nuzzle me until my purr's so loud you get a ticket for disturbing the peace."

Once the cat was pacified, it didn't take long to draw the lines necessary to turn Aaron Meckler's "starscape" into a facsimile of a molecule. We hoped we had gotten it right, its appearance meant no more to us than the schematic of a heart valve machine.

"Maybe we should have made another copy of the print before we started drawing all over this one?" Charles suggested about an hour too late.

"I can make a smaller one off my printer," I picked up my iPhone and opened the email app so I could print the attachment Adrianne sent. It wasn't there. "Can't be."

Charles pulled out his cell phone and did the same, with the same result.

"How the hell?" I asked. "Three cell phones, three copies of exactly the same picture missing?"

"We've been hacked," said my neighborhood computer expert.

"By whom?"

"Sebastian? Really?"

"Markham and his henchmen?"

"Who else?"

"But we still have two hard copies. This one here, and the one back at the studio. Uh oh, we may have a problem." I said, as I called up Adrianne's number on my phone. Her phone rang and rang and rang; and then went to voice mail.

"My car," Charles said before I could ask the question. "I can get there faster. Most DPD know me."

He cut the time back to the gallery by a third. We never had to test how well-liked he might be by DPD, so there was no stopping. And the driving skills he learned when he was a cop back in Palm Springs, paid off big time.

Charles took the turn into the alley a little too fast and, but for the seat belts we were wearing, we would have clunked our heads on the roof of his Beamer.

The back door to the gallery was standing open. But it was a warm day for the season, and that didn't mean there was anything wrong. Still, we approached with caution, trying to see inside the gallery. The difference in ambient lighting, and the clutter of Adrianne's backroom, kept us from seeing more than a few feet inside.

Neither of us were armed, but Charles' police training, and superior size, dictated he enter first. I was right on his heels, looking around him and mentally trying to get my eyes to adjust to the dimmer light of the gallery.

It was so quiet, you could have heard the stroke of a paintbrush. But there was no one. No shuffling of art, good natured camaraderie, or a carelessly dropped object. It was still as a mannequin's breath.

Charles suddenly lunged forward and dropped to one knee. I came around his side to see him checking for a pulse on the thick neck of one Eugene Spielberg, AKA, Horse.

"How is he?" I asked with genuine concern for this huge man with the kind heart.

"A lesser man would be dead, but he's going to be all right. Looks like someone tried to strangle him with a length of aircraft cable." Charles and I looked up at the material Adrianne used to hang the panels for her paintings. Then we looked around and saw several lengths of the cable on the floor around us. "He also had the presence of mind to jam pliers up between his neck and the cable. I'm guessing he was just taking too long to die. And whoever did this, wanted to get the hell away from here before he was seen. Call 911 Sebastian," Charles said redundantly, as I already had my phone to my ear.

After making sure the cable was loose enough for Horse to breathe, Charles left the man exactly as he found him, not wanting to possibly cause further damage, and probably wanting the crime scene to be as pristine as possible. Sirens were approaching fast as I swung up the stairs searching for Adrianne, fearing the worst.

Since all the clutter of paintings that cramped the upstairs were now downstairs in the gallery, the place seemed almost bare. A quick look around told me there was no one vertical in the room. I checked the floor for a limp body, or some evidence of a struggle. Nothing. Same in the bathroom and out on the balcony. I did another quick once-through, even checked under the bed. Nothing.

"How are you feeling?" I heard Charles ask Horse as I came down the stairs slowly, still looking around for Adrianne or any clue as to what happened.

"Don't think I'll be drinking whiskey any time soon," the larger man understated.

"Can you sit up?" Charles asked. Then to me, "Sebastian, bring a glass of water."

I drew a cup of water from the cooler near the back door and brought it over. Horse took it from my hand, a good sign. He sipped, massaged his throat gently. "Glad it's you," he said to me, then looked at Charles.

"Charles Love," I explained to Horse. "Computer maven, neighbor, good guy, good friend."

"Wish it was under better circumstances," Charles said as Horse took a larger drink. "Can you tell us what happened? Where's Adrianne?"

Horse pointed with the cup of water to a piece of torn paper on the floor near him. I picked it up. It was the torn quarter corner of the color print of Aaron Meckler's painting. The other three quarters of the piece were nowhere in evidence. Horse made a kind of circular motion with his cup hand.

I turned the paper over. "She will call you. Be alone," was the message written on the back in the black ink of a ballpoint pen.

"There was a man in the doorway," Horse said in the

halting voice of someone who had gargled kitchen cleanser. He motioned toward the back door. "Adrianne just said, 'Shit.' I ran toward him. As soon as I got to the door, one of his guys came at me from the side, I turned, and another guy hit me over the head with a pipe or something. The two of them pushed me back into the gallery, got me down and started to choke me with a piece of cable. I managed to get pliers from my pocket and wedge them here," he indicated the area between his collarbone and his jaw. "It helped, I guess, but I still blacked out."

"Probably saved your life," I said, as paramedics came through the front door, followed by Sergeant Rawlins. I hadn't realized it wasn't locked. I quickly crumpled the paper in my hand and shoved it into my pocket. I think Horse saw me do it, and that he winked his approval, but it might just have been a wince of pain.

"And," I wanted to cut to the chase before Rawlins could, "they left with Adrianne?"

The big man nodded his confirmation, and his understanding that we might not want to let the cops know just yet. He didn't have a lot of faith in the police. And, despite his current and former professions, Charles wasn't thoroughly enamored with their achievements either.

By the time we left the gallery, nearly an hour later, Horse was vertical, drinking a cup of soothing tea, and refusing further medical attention—probably due to less than desirable finances and his distrust of the law. He told Rawlins everything he told us. That is, every word that he had spoken. He omitted his hand gestures, winks, nods and pointing; as well as the results of those subtle machinations. In other words, they knew three men had come into the gallery, and now they, and Adrianne, were nowhere to be found. All absolutely true.

We lingered on after the EMTs, Rawlins and the other police left, suggesting that we would help Horse get things back in order, and assuring the skeptical sergeant that each of us would certainly call if there was any news or other information we could impart.

As the last of their vehicles pulled away from the curb, Charles pulled out his phone and asked Horse, "Did one of the men look like . . . Damn."

I knew exactly what had happened and clicked my phone to life only to find that Dwight Markham's internet picture was gone.

Chapter 24

"Hack me, will they?" Charles said. "Those sons of bitches don't know who they're messing with."

"Horse," I said. "Can you lock up here? We gotta get going."

"Sure man."

"Don't forget to set the alarm," I said, then to Charles, "Back to your place?"

"Nope. But let's get going."

"What've you got in mind?" I asked as soon as we were in the car.

"Need some quiet time to work this out," he said, louder than necessary, as if he wanted someone else to hear. He steered his car in the opposite direction of our homes. Made a turn at normal speed and gave me a quick look and a nod when the car had straightened out; the combined, silent gestures came through to me even louder than his previous spoken remarks. It said, "Don't ask questions, just follow my lead." He slipped Paul Horn's "Inside" into the CD slot and said, unnecessarily, "Horn recorded this inside the Taj Mahal in the '60s. Still the best meditation music there is. Helps me think. I'm just going to pull into the parking lot at City Park where the Museum of Nature and Science is and listen while I let my little gray cells come up with something."

His words were completely out of character for the

dynamic, quick thinker I knew him to be. But he wanted me to go along with it, "I'm good with that," I said.

"Yeah, but're you okay with just letting the juices flow? You know, stream of consciousness. Not forcing it. Just being perfectly quiet and letting your brain work things out?" He shot that look at me again.

"Sure, I've done that before."

Charles pulled the BMW into a lot as far away from the museum as possible. He cut the engine, but left the accessories on so the CD kept playing. He cracked the windows on the front about a quarter of an inch. Then he reached into his pocket, pulled out his cell phone and put it under his seat. He indicated that I should do the same. "Wait here, I'm going to go over to that Port-a-potty and take a leak," I didn't see any Port-a-potties anywhere, but didn't say anything. He got out of the car and closed the driver's door. He leaned against the car for about two-and-a-half minutes. Then he came over to my side and opened the door. "That's much better," he said. "You need to go?" he asked, as he shook his head and motioned for me to get out.

"No, I'm good," I said, sliding out of my seat. Charles closed the door, locked it with his remote and we walked over to Colorado Boulevard.

Confident that traffic noise on the busy thoroughfare would mask our speech, he finally said, "Heading over to my sister's home, just across the street."

"You think they could hear our conversation through our cell phones?" I let him know my paranoid suspicions.

"Gotta think that if they can get into our emails and photos and eliminate specific pictures, they've figured out how to hear us, even when our phones are 'off,' so to speak. They're probably tracking us through the GPS, too."

"So leaving the phones in the car with Paul Horn and all that *mishegas* about meditating on the matter was just so we can't be heard?"

"That's part of it."

"And the fake pissing was to cover for the sound of the car door closing, twice?"

"You pretty smart, for a journalist," he paraphrased a line from some long-forgotten movie, which probably really said "You pretty smart for a white boy." I wasn't offended.

Five houses in from Colorado Boulevard, Charles walked up the concrete walkway of a classic, brick bungalow with a second story that, though added, had been professionally done and blended seamlessly with the original house. He pulled his keychain from his pocket and said, as he opened the front door, "My sister's place."

"The one who works at Denver Health?"

"Yeah. She and her husband will be at work right now. Kids are in school."

"So, a real quiet place for us to do some serious brain storming?"

"Not exactly."

"She has a good computer you can use to hack the hacker?"

"She don't know beans about computers. But I gave my niece a state-of-the-art machine for Christmas that'll blow the keys off anything off the shelf."

"Excellent."

We made our way upstairs to a too-pink bedroom. Charles sat at a desk looking like some giant at a little girl's tea party. He flipped open his niece's laptop and spoke as he poked the keys and fingered the track pad. "This dufus has created a roadway into our phones, including Adrianne's and probably your new friend Elizabeth Brown. He may have even got into Terri's phone. His problem is that, any reasonably intelligent person knows that a roadway goes both ways, if you get my meaning. We can backtrack his footprints from our phones to his. Which, among other things, will tell us where he is right now.."

"You mean, where his phone is right now. Not necessarily where he is."

"Only if he's better at this than I am. He isn't."

"But, doesn't that raise the question of what happens if Adrianne, or Markham using Adrianne's phone, tries to call me right now? My phone's locked in your car."

"The first thing I did when I got here was to forward your phone to Shatze's computer."

"Your niece?"

"Her nickname. Yeah, you've met her."

"You've got a big family."

He smiled, "Yeah. Anyway, we were out of cell phone communication for less than five minutes. It was a calculated risk that needed to be taken. I'm gonna be borrowing Shatze's computer, so if the call from Markham comes through while we're on our way back to the car, we're covered. Okay, got him," Charles said.

"Offices of Prefaxal Pharmaceuticals? Downtown or Denver Tech Center?" I projected.

"No, warehouse on Jason Street. Not all that far from AM Gallery. Makes sense. Probably have fancy offices downtown or DTC, but they'd need manufacturing and warehousing facilities somewhere. Taking her there isn't the brightest move."

"Neither is trying to make millions by hurting people."

"Touché."

"The smart move would be to alert Rawlins," I said half-heartedly

"Who says we smart? Besides, they'd need to get a search warrant and all that legal paraphernalia. We don't have time for that. Give me a second to finish up here. We need to get back to my car."

As we quick-walked back to Charles' car he said, "Open your door and slide in quietly. Don't close the door until I'm in my seat. I'll say something and then turn the key in the ignition. When the starter motor engages, we'll both close our doors. I think the noise from the starter will cover the sound from the doors closing."

"Where to from here?" I asked as we crossed Colorado Boulevard.

"Makes sense to go back to your place. That shouldn't raise any red flags. We'll just wait there until they call. Don't think we'll have to wait long."

"What's the plan?" I asked.

"You're going to go wherever they ask you to in your car. I'll leave my phone at your place, but I'll follow you in my car. You've used your phone to record interviews?" he asked.

"Of course. I can even turn it to record in my pocket, if I've set it up beforehand."

"I want you to do just that, before you actually meet them. Maybe before you get out of your car. You know, everything we've got so far is circumstantial?"

"Except for kidnapping Adrianne," I replied.

"Yeah, that. That's where he really messed up. He thinks he can get away with anything. Probably figuring on some way to kill you both and make it look like a murder/suicide. A variation on his usual M.O."

We had stopped to talk about 20 feet from his BMW to ensure traffic noise from the boulevard masked our conversation.

"You mean the way he murdered Chaffee, probably after hiring him to murder Aaron Meckler and Marvin Saines." I said.

"That's the way I see it," Charles said.

"I'm with you. But not so sure about more murders, specifically mine and Adrianne's."

"Like I said. He thinks he's too smart to get caught."

"You think that in addition to feeling certain he can get away with two more murders, and bring a dangerous drug to market, he'll boast to me and Adrianne about how he got rid of the threats from Saines and Meckler, and murdered Chaffee? And, maybe how he's going to get rid of us?" I asked uncomfortably.

"That's about the size of it."

"And you want me to get it all recorded on my phone?" I was incredulous.

"Yep," he said continuing toward the car. "I don't see any other way we can get the evidence we need for the murders he's committed, and the fraud and abuse he's about to commit with his fat pill."

We were about 10 feet from the car. I was processing what he just said at lightning speed. Damn, he was right. "Okay, but you're going to be listening in all the time? You've got our backs, right?

"Absolutely," he produced an old flip phone from his pocket. "Can't be hacked with the gear he's using. We'll just keep an old fashioned open line on between us. When the time comes, I'll call Rawlins. We'll have probable cause, and she can bring in the cavalry."

"Good." His plan was simple and straightforward.

It sounded to me like we pulled off the delicate ballet of BMW door closure. I hoped I wasn't being too optimistic.

Charles carefully stowed his niece's computer between his bucket seat and the shift consol. He started up some chatter as we headed back toward our homes in the Highlands. "You probably don't want to hear this," he said. "But I think they've got you over a barrel. It's not like they're asking you for millions of dollars. Just a piece of paper with a picture of a crappy painting, in exchange for your girlfriend."

I pretended to resist and we bantered back and forth for nearly 20 minutes until he pulled up to the garage behind his house. Getting out and heading toward my townhome I said, "Screw it. Okay. I'll get the painting and wait for the goddamn call. Come over if you want."

Charles grinned, but said in an argumentative tone, "Go get it. I've gotta get something. I'll be over in a few minutes."

***

True to his word, Charles showed up within five minutes. Motley had wolfed down some wet food and was getting adored by his human when Charles came through the back door, gun in hand.

He held it out without saying a word. Motley saw it and slunk away under a kitchen chair. I shook my head. He knew I wasn't into guns, but it was nice of him to offer. He double-checked the safety and tucked it away in a pocket. "I guess we just wait," he said. Motley came out from under the chair slowly and returned to his human for comforting.

Chapter 25

My cell phone seemed to ring right on cue. As expected, the caller ID was Adrianne Meckler. Also as expected, I was told to bring every copy of the print of the picture of the painting to a warehouse on Jason Street. By his syntax and tone, I figured it was Dwight Markham himself. He reiterated that I was to bring any and all copies. And, that I was to come alone. "There's just the one," I told him. He hung up as if to say, "There better not be any more."

I was getting very nervous. I clicked my phone off, but Charles put his hand out for it. As I gave it to him I realized I hadn't preset it to record. He did it for me.

"You okay to drive?" he asked.

"I better be. You can't be my chauffeur."

"You're right. It wouldn't look right," he grinned. "It's going to be okay. I'll be right here," he said, as he gently laid his digital cell phone down on the kitchen counter so Markham would think he was still at the house. Then, he patted his other pocket to remind me that he would be listening to my every move on the old analog phone they couldn't hack.

We left through the back door at the same time, so there would only be the sound of one door closing. He walked up to his house and got into his car. We started our vehicles at almost the same moment, continuously cautious about the sounds we might be making. I kept him in my rearview mirror as I negotiated the roads and traffic between the Highlands and the warehouses down on Jason Street. He parked about 300 feet away from the address I was headed for. I had a lump in my throat as if I just swallowed a whole orange.

On legs made of Jell-O, I ascended the eight concrete steps to the glass door in the huge gray building. The only weapons I had were a rolled up piece of 11x17 paper with a strange picture on it, and a cell phone I activated to start recording. Suddenly, I felt I was up against the Broncos' defensive line wearing only a jock strap.

I went through the doorway. There was an outer office with only one very large man. I didn't recognize his face, but his build seemed to be the same as one of the two men who bullied and pushed their way into the gallery to steal the original painting by Aaron Meckler. As I approached, I got a whiff of stale tobacco. I recognized the obnoxious odor from the night before. I was sure the other one wasn't far away.

He turned without a word and walked through another doorway. I understood I was to follow. What bones were left in my legs seemed to be melting away.

On the other side of the door, we entered an enormous warehouse full of shelving. Over to one side were walls, behind which, I assumed, were labs and the equipment necessary to produce a wide variety of pills, capsules, and potions. At the rear of the building were enormous doors that opened vertically. When I saw them, my mind wandered aimlessly to the fact that the warehouses in this part of Denver backed to railroad tracks to facilitate loading and unloading freight.

I snapped my brain back to the scenario at hand. Big, tough, tobacco-stink guy was heading toward a door in the inner building that I understood to be the labs, manufacturing and packaging space. My mind wandered again: are they going to try to shoot us? There would be no sound heard outside this building. Maybe shoot one and hang the other? Dire thoughts. Have to focus. Remain calm. Have faith in Charles' plan, whatever it is.

Tobacco Breath opened the door and waited. I walked through it expecting to see Adrianne tied to a chair with a gag in her mouth—she was just sitting in a chair in front of a desk, her skin tone ashen. Behind the desk was an older, grayer version of the internet photo Charles had of Dwight Markham. Sitting comfortably on another chair in a corner, where a solid wall met a wall with a shaded window, was the other big, tough guy. His calculated position commanded a view of the entire room and its two doors. Stacked against the solid wall to his right, I recognized gas tanks like the ones in the horse barn where PC Chaffee had been rendered unconscious with chloroform before being hanged.

Markham came out from behind the desk so he was just a few feet from me. Leaning back on the executive furniture, he motioned to my escort. Tobacco Breath moved my arms out from my sides like some spastic marionette, and frisked me. He passed on my wallet and keys but pulled my phone from my pocket. He held it out to Markham. Markham shook his head. Tobacco Breath dropped my very expensive iPhone on the concrete floor, and smashed it like a cheap, plastic toy. He bent over and pulled the sim card from the detritus and put it in his pocket. It could just as easily have been my beating heart for all the fear I felt.

"Now we can speak freely, Mr. Wren," Markham said. I was screwed. No recording. No evidence. No link to Charles. No hope. "This thing in your hand," he indicated the rolled up print. I had completely forgotten about it. "It's really the only copy? I can't believe that."

My angst was draining like water in a canal, and quickly being replaced by anger and adrenalin. I had to keep it under control. There may yet be a way out of this. Just keep him talking. There's two of us. If we can make it out alive, we can corroborate each other. If we can salvage the print, better yet. And, maybe, with luck, the painting was somewhere in this building. Or we could find it at Markham's home or office. Stay calm. "As I told you on the phone, we didn't think to make another print. We had plenty of backups on our phones."

"Ah yes, the phones. Well, I guess we took care of those for you. Yes, even Ms. Brown's."

"You know there are too many people who are on to you for you to get away with this," I said boldly, my pastiche of confidence was beginning to add color to Adrianne's face.

"Not very likely," he responded, deflating my courage and dialing Adrianne's skin tone back a notch. "You see, in addition to deleting certain files from all your phones and computers, I've been listening in on your conversations for the last 15 hours. Neat little toys you and your friends have. I know that you came here from your house in the Highlands. And, earlier today, you and Mr. Love were parked in City Park for nearly 20 minutes. Also, I know that he is at your house waiting to hear something incriminating from your phone while it's recording our little talk, so he can call in the police at the appropriate moment. Incidentally, I know that Elizabeth Brown is at work at her little magazine right now. She's no problem. We can scoop her up at any time. Have I left anyone out?"

"Don't forget my cat," I hissed in tribute to my feline.

"Oh yes, your precious Maine Coon. Don't worry, we'll take him to the Cat Care Society after we take care of Charles and Terri Love. Now, does that cover everyone?"

"By my count, that would make eight murders." I said. Trying to reign in my temper was like pulling back on a team of panicked Clydesdales.

"Eight, really? You, your girlfriends Adrianne and Elizabeth, their kin, Meckler and Saines, your neighbors,

Charles and Terri. That's only seven. Oh yes, that moron PC Chaffee. You're right, eight. So sad."

I was starting to feel a little better, I was getting what I needed to incriminate this miscreant. Now all I had to do was get Adrianne and me out alive.

"Yes, so sad. Are you going to feel equally sad about the thousands you're going to injure and kill with your new fat pill?"

"Ah yes, you figured it all out, didn't you. It's just business, Sebastian. May I call you Sebastian?" He went on without waiting for an answer, "You see, in business there are calculated risks. My people assure me that the numbers who might be harmed by Plavynia probably wouldn't have lived very long anyhow."

"Plavynia?" I said.

"That's the name marketing came up with for what you call our fat pill.
Pretty catchy, isn't it? Anyway, as I was saying, the numbers who might not benefit from Plavynia are probably already in poor health. Many of them smoke, have diabetes and are at risk of a stroke or heart disease. Most have a poor diet and terrible genes. Meanwhile, we'll be helping hundreds of thousands . . ."

"At profits that are worth billions."

"Yes, there is that."

"That makes you a parasite, as well as a sociopath," Adrianne put in.

"Indeed, you are your father's daughter," Markham turned to her. "He was going to take that dreadful painting to the FDA and have them connect the dots, literally and figuratively."

"Which would show that the formula you're using for your drug is different than the one you submitted with your paperwork," I said. "Minor differences, if I understand it correctly, but significant in that one is safe but doesn't help people lose weight, while the other is effective in both weight loss and killing people."

"Really Sebastian, so melodramatic?"

"The FDA *will* find out, and you will be ruined," Adrianne seethed.

"Fat chance," Markham said. "The government turns its back on corporate culpability all the time. With the help of the media, the public's attention gets misdirected better than by a magician in Las Vegas. On the one hand, the public panics when there is one case of Ebola in the country, while they turn their heads and ignore the epidemic of diabetes caused by the added sugar in processed foods, which is killing thousands more every year than Plavynia ever will. Why? Company profits. Corporate donations to politicians. In a word: lobbying.

"What about the fear of marijuana because someone jumps out a window after eating too many pot-laced cookies? Meanwhile, alcohol flows freely as tens of thousands die every year from it every year.

"And it seems there's always some tainted food scare, like cantaloupes with salmonella because people didn't wash them or their knives. And suddenly tons of fruit went rotting on the vine, bankrupting small farmers. Meanwhile, the NRA, AKA the gun lobby, successfully shuts down gun safety legislation while tens of thousands of US citizens are killed in shootings every year.

"Do you really think a few deaths from Plavynia, most of which our lawyers can successfully defend, are going to keep the government or the public from wanting the drug? Americans are not alone in wanting a way to lose weight by just taking a pill. And, they're not alone in thinking that it, whatever malignant thing *it* may be, will never happen to them."

"You're really one sick son-of-a-bitch," Adrianne said.

"Just like your father, and that simpleton McIntosh. If

only we could have gotten to him in prison . . ."

I noticed a small, low shadow cross outside the shaded outside window. It appeared to be the top of someone's head. Charles? I had hope.

"What about Marvin Saines and PC Chaffee?" I asked, as much to stall as to get him to explain and confess.

"Saines was good. Too good. He crunched the numbers and talked with the lawyers. But, like the judge, he wanted us to kill the project."

"But you decided to let the project live and kill the consumer. Along with Saines."

"Cute, Wren. But any of those people could die at any time, from anything. Have a flower pot fall on their heads, get hit by a bus. Life's a risk. Grow up."

"And Chaffee?"

"Now there's someone who could fuck up a wet dream. He pulled off killing Saines and Meckler." At the mention of her father's murder, Adrianne turned scarlet and moved forward in her seat to lunge at Markham. Big tough guy put one big hand on her shoulder and shoved her back down in her chair. "But he screwed up big time when he tried to torch the gallery. Again, if he had been successful, if the gallery burned along with that painting, we wouldn't be here now. I knew it was only a matter of time before the police would track him down. Unfortunately for you, Sebastian, you got to him before I could make a clean getaway. But, all was not lost. My people were scanning police communications and found no mention of me, my car, or my appearance, so I knew I had gotten away clean."

"Except for coming to the gallery the day you tried to buy Dad's painting," Adrianne gloated a little.

"Yes," I added. "And, if you had done nothing at all after Aaron Meckler's death, no one would have been any the wiser about the painting. You're not so brilliant after all."

That finally got under his skin and he backhanded me

across my cheek. He had at least 25 pounds on me and I crumpled to the floor. A moment later a large black former cop burst through the door. Charles' gun was drawn, but he hadn't identified his targets. Adrianne got up quick from her chair. The tough guy behind her shoved her down while using the same momentum to propel himself toward Charles. I twisted my body on the floor and managed to get my legs entangled with Tobacco Breath. He fell forward right in front of Charles. Charles tripped on the man's body but managed to grab Markham. Both men fell hard to the ground, Charles' gun came loose and slid across the floor in my direction.

I grabbed the piece, rolled onto my side as I cocked the hammer and got a shot off that blasted through the leg of the tough guy. As soon as the man hit the floor, Tobacco Breath grabbed my wrist just behind the gun, and yanked it back. There was a popping sound that was my rotator cuff. I screamed in pain and dropped the gun. Adrianne lunged for it. But Tobacco Breath was on his feet and put one foot down on her advancing arm. He reached down for the gun and spoke for the first time, "Everyone just lay very still while Mr. Markham gets up. First one to move is dead. Mr. Markham, sir. Please check this new guy for any weapons or phones."

Markham bent over Charles and did a half-assed pat down. This wasn't his normal role. There weren't any other weapons, but he did find Charles' old flip phone. More in anger than for security, the Prefaxal CEO dropped the phone to the floor in front of Charles's face and stomped on it four times, reducing it to a pile of rubble with one remaining, blinking LED.

I thought I saw a smile cross Charles' face. But then it was gone.

Chapter 26

Charles, Adrianne and I were pulled up and shoved about until we were all seated in office chairs. The pain in my right shoulder was excruciating, but I didn't want to wince or whine and give them the satisfaction of knowing how badly I was hurt, as if they gave a damn. A length of familiar-looking rope with a greenish tinge now held each of us in place. Wounded tough guy was in a fourth chair, his only bindings were the bandages from the warehouse's first aid kit, which were keeping him from bleeding to death. He was out of commission. I tried to tell myself that now it was two of them, and three of us; we had them out numbered. Except they had guns and we were tied to chairs. Of course, now they had the problem of getting rid of us, preferably somewhere other than here.

"Mr. Markham," Tobacco Breath said, "how about I bring one of the delivery trucks up to the front loading dock. We wheel them in and I'll drive out somewhere where nobody'll find 'em?"

Markham thought about that for half a second. "No. You never know who's out there. Besides, someone in here is bound to see us wheeling out people tied to chairs and call the cops."

Just then I heard the slow clatter of heavy steel wheels rolling over railroad track joints, accompanied by vibrations that came up through the building's foundation and rippled across the concrete floors. Markham lit up, "Someone's getting a delivery. That means part of the train will be right out back. We can just open one of the bay doors, find a box car with a little extra space and put them in."

"What about them talking when they're found?" Tobacco Breath asked.

"They won't be in any condition to talk."

"One shot each?"

"One front, one back. Both to the head. I want to make sure this time. We'll put them in the freight car first, that way there won't be any blood or DNA around here. Their bodies won't be found until they reach Kansas, or Utah, depending on where the train goes next.

"Wheel them over by the doors. We'll use the chloroform. Knock them out one at a time. Cut them loose from their chairs, and tie them back up."

I tried not to breathe in the anesthesia. But I could only hold my breath for about a minute. The next thing I knew, I was lying on the floor of the warehouse near the huge vertical doors along with Charles and Adrianne. Each of us trussed up like pigs, ready for a barbecue. Fright filled Adrianne's eyes. Charles seemed to be doing all right. Maybe it was his police training, some Zen Buddhist practices he dabbled in, or just accepting his fate, but he seemed oddly at ease. Or, maybe like me, he was puzzled, seeing the whole situation as an observer, trying to figure out a way to get loose and overpower our captors.

"Ready boss?"

"Go ahead and unlock the door. There's plenty of noise out there to cover us.
But, don't open them all the way, just enough to get them out and onto the train.

Tobacco Breath released the locking mechanism and pushed a big green button to raise the metal door. The door jerked up an inch when the motor engaged. Then it began a smooth, if noisy, ascent. From my trussed-up position on the floor of the warehouse, a reddish-brown box car came into view. Its huge sliding door fully opened as if the old railroad car had been ordered up special. What I was sure would be our oversized coffin, was now ready to swallow us up whole.

Tobacco Breath pressed an even larger red button that brought the warehouse door to a halt at about six feet. He and Markham looked at each other and the open maw of the freight car. Markham said, "Now isn't that convenient. Let's take the big one first."

Markham leaned over and grabbed Charles' feet as Tobacco Breath leaned in to clutch the big man's shoulders.

At that moment, Detective Sergeant Frankie Rawlins stepped out of the shadows of the freight car and into its open doorway. She was quickly surrounded by a dozen of Denver's finest. Kevlar vests in place. Rifles pointed into the warehouse. "Set him down nice and easy," she said.

The two men complied. Police streamed out of the freight car and into the warehouse as Rawlins bent down and sliced open our bonds with a retractable, razor-sharp knife. First Adrianne, then me, then Charles. Adrianne and Charles got to their feet, rubbing their wrists. I rolled onto my side and managed to get into a sitting position, holding my right shoulder with my left hand. The adrenalin was ebbing, the pain was flowing.

The other policemen and women quickly found the wounded tough guy and handcuffed him, as they had his partners in crime. People from the front office and other facilities were rounded up. But Charles and Adrianne assured Rawlins they were not involved. Names and vitals were taken, and they were told to leave the building—as this was now an official crime scene—but not to leave town.

"You don't have any real proof of anything," Markham said to us when Rawlins was out of ear shot, though not out of sight. "I've got plenty of corporate money and the best lawyers, I'll be back in business in a month."

"We have all the proof we need," Charles said. "In fact, a full recorded confession."

"You're bluffing. We destroyed your phones. You've got nothing."

I winced back the pain so I could take pleasure in the explaining. "True, you destroyed our phones and our ability to record you on them. But Charles reversed your hack. He was recording you onto his niece's laptop . . . from your phone."

Charles continued as the pain overtook me, "When you hacked me, you opened a gateway into your phone. All of your information and your conversations from the last couple of hours are now safely archived on my niece's cute, little, pink laptop."

Adrianne beamed and threw her arms first around Charles, and then me. "Ouch," I screamed and toppled over on my side.

"We gotta get you to the hospital, again," she said.

Chapter 27

Rawlins had ordered up a couple of ambulances, anticipating casualties. There were only two: me, and the wounded tough guy.

I lost at least one full day. A few hours were from my surgery. The rest was recovering from anesthesia and an abundance of pain pills. I finally came to on Terri Love's watch. Apparently she, Charles and Elizabeth Brown had been trading off being nearby during the day. Adrianne was on deadline to get the gallery set up for her big opening. I understood.

"What day is it?" I asked my friend and neighbor.

"You're supposed to tell us. It's a sign that there's no brain damage. Though, because it's you, it wouldn't prove a thing," Terri teased. "It's Thursday."

"Morning or afternoon?"

"Early afternoon."

"And?"

"And, if everything checks out, you can go home as soon as you show them you can walk to the bathroom by yourself."

"I'm ready for my big test."

Nurses and doctors came and went over the next two hours. First having me stand. Then disconnecting catheters and tubes, and having me walk down the hall and back with my IV stand. Satisfied that neither my leg injuries from

earlier in the week, or my healing shoulder—and the meds
that were holding back the pain—were keeping me from
being vertical, they allowed me to check out of the hospital.
So long as I promised not to operate any heavy equipment
or drive for at least a week. Deal.

Terri took me for a great big fat bacon-cheeseburger with
fries and a Pepsi. And that was just going to get me through
to dinner. She fixed up the couch in my living room so I
could watch TV and sleep. Motley was glad to curl up
behind my bruised legs and help lull me off. "I'll bring over
some dinner around six. You think you'll be up for
company? There's a few people that want to see you with
your eyes open. And Charles says there's some unfinished
business to take care of."

"Yeah. I'd like that," I was looking forward to seeing
Adrianne, as well as the rest of the folks that had been
wrapped up in this mess.

***

Terri showed up at five as I was watching the news.
Between all the *mishegas* of the past week, and my stay in the
hospital, I'd been away from my evening news fix for quite a
while. Nothing had changed. Fuck it.

"Thought I'd come by and help you get cleaned up a bit?"

"You going to give me a sponge bath?"

"In your dreams. I'm just going to make sure you don't
fall down those stairs when you go up for your shower."

"What if I slip and fall in the shower."

"Then I'll call 911 and get some big, ugly, male EMT to
carry you downstairs."

"I'll be careful."

Charles was downstairs when I emerged from my shower.
As I descended the stairs, Adrianne entered. She looked
tired, but happy. "Sebastian," she said, "I'm so glad to see
you. Charles has been keeping me in the loop. How're you
feeling? Sorry for the way I look. I haven't had time to clean

177

up, eat or sleep. The show's tomorrow. But, I'm almost there."

"Thanks for coming over, Adrianne. You better get some rest before tomorrow. If I know you, everything's perfect and you're just overthinking it. Relax. Let it be. Go home after dinner, soak in your tub, and get a good night's sleep."

She looked like some guru had just given her the meaning of life, or permission to just be herself—same thing. "Yeah, you're right. I'm an artist. Rules don't apply."

I reached the bottom of the stairs as Elizabeth let herself in. I refrained from hugging anyone, lest it put undo pressure on my arm. Terri went back to her place and returned with baked chicken, roasted potatoes and salad. All things I could eat left-handed. I appreciated it.

Over dinner everyone helped catch me up. Markham and both tough guys were still in jail and would be facing arraignment Friday morning. Adrianne wondered if they would get out on bail. Conventional wisdom said they would, given Prefaxal's deep pockets.

Adrianne also wanted to know how Rawlins managed to get the freight car lined up perfectly with the warehouse door?

"Sebastian and I had anticipated Markham taking away our phones and disabling them."

"You mean you planned to get caught?" Terri was incredulous, and angry.

"We had to, hon," Charles said. "We needed to make it look like an act of desperation, so he could gloat. We knew that if he thought he had gotten away with murder, and the duplicity of his fat pill plan, he would tell all."

"We're still gonna have a little talk, mister ex-cop, IT-whiz, hero. So now tell us all about how you outwitted this Markham character and got your police friend to rescue you."

"Well, given Markham's proclivity for violence, we

anticipated him destroying my analog phone. So, when he trashed Sebastian's iPhone, we knew we had him. I called Detective Rawlins and told her where we were and what we had engineered."

"And she was good with that?" Terri said.

"Absolutely not. But it was too late for her to stop it. And, there was no time for her to bawl me out or argue. I built a micro transmitter small enough to go into my sock, just above my shoe. It has bluetooth capability, so it can transmit my exact GPS location, but only up to 30 feet. I also connected a tiny transceiver to the battery of my analog phone that would relay the signal from the transmitter in my sock to the GPS in Rawlins' phone. When my analog phone got smashed, it triggered the transceiver to relay the signal from the device in my sock, so Rawlins and DPD would know precisely where I was."

"What's going to happen to Doctor McIntosh?" Elizabeth Brown wanted to know.

"For now," Charles said, "he has to remain in custody. But he's been apprised of the situation and his spirits are up. His children were also brought into the loop, unofficially, of course, and they're arranging to visit him soon. But his fate really depends on what happens with Markham and Prefaxal."

"Isn't there anything that can be done about that bastard?" Adrianne asked.

"I've got a couple of ideas," I said. "But it might just be the pain killers talking."

"We're listening," Charles said.

"First off, did Rawlins find the original painting?" I asked.

"Yes," Charles said. "They're holding it as evidence in the assault charges they're bringing on behalf of you, me and Adrianne. Also, clear proof of theft. But not murder."

"Damn. I was hoping we could get the painting to the FDA to prove malfeasance. Maybe there's some other way we can keep them in jail?" I said. It was more thinking out loud than an actual question.

"To paraphrase that putz Markham, 'Fat fucking chance,'" Adrianne said. She and Elizabeth looked like they had lost a winning lottery ticket.

"I think I've got it," I said. "All the evidence for murder is circumstantial at this point."

"Even with the confession?" Adrianne asked.

"Since we recorded them surreptitiously," Charles put in, "it won't carry enough weight to hold them for now. But it will count as evidence at their trials."

"Eventually," I continued, "Rawlins and the crime scene unit will tie it all together. Finger prints on chloroform canisters, specific make of rope, phone records, etc. But, by the time that gels, Markham will be in some country with no extradition . . ."

"Living off the millions he's made making dangerous knock off drugs and selling them into third world countries . . ." Charles picked up on my train of thought.

"Right. DPD may not be able to keep them in jail without bail, right now, but if there's some way we can keep them from posting bail . . ."

"I think I see where you're going . . ." Charles said.

"Can you pull it off?" I asked.

"I can do the nuts and bolts, or ones and zeroes. Can you do the creative?" he asked.

"Yeah, I got an idea."

"Let's do it," Charles said. He picked up the cute, little, pink laptop he had expropriated from his niece and started for my study. I got up slowly, my arm still aching, despite the pain killers. I followed him in and closed the double doors.

It was almost an hour later when we emerged from my inner sanctum.

"You two look like cats that just ate canaries," Terri said.

"What've you been up to?"

"You don't want to know," the big man said, pink laptop in hand.

"*Oh yes we do,*" Terri gave us a look.

Charles looked at me.

"Okay," I said, sitting down on the couch with Terri and Elizabeth. "Hypothetically: What do you suppose would happen if a low level state department person at a US embassy in a third-world country sent an email to the D.O.J. inquiring about the status of an investigation of inferior drugs that appear to have caused many illnesses, suffering and even deaths in said country? And, what if there were some national media asking questions about why personnel from the company involved are still out walking the streets and doing business as usual?"

"I wonder what that could lead to," Terri said.

"You mean, like immediately freezing a company's assets, so officers couldn't pay employees, rent, mortgages, bank loans, . . . and incidentals?"

"Incidentals? Like bail?" Elizabeth asked impishly.

"I wouldn't know." I said.

***

Before she left, Adrianne asked me to join her in the kitchen for a moment. "Sebastian," she said. "This has really been a hell of a week. I'm so glad we met. And, that we're friends." I just stood there listening. The painkillers were slowing things in my brain, especially something appropriate, or even inappropriate, to say.

"You see," she went on, "while you were in the hospital . .. well ...I ... I met someone. He's very nice. You'll like him. And, well, we've been together the last few days. He's been helping at the gallery after he gets off work, and, well . .."

Her many pauses and slow delivery gave me the time I needed to say, "Hey, it's all good. You seem very happy, and

181

I'm happy for you."

"Thanks Sebastian. See you tomorrow night?"

"Absolutely."

***

My morning TV news program came on with breaking news that was actually breaking news. It was a report that a Colorado pharmaceutical company's CEO was arrested for knowingly distributing potentially deadly drugs to foreign countries, some of which were finding their way back into the US. It went on to say that he was already in jail on unrelated charges. His company's assets had been frozen by the Justice Department. And, he was being held without bail. While newscast "Ken and Barbie" only got about 75 percent of the story correct, it warmed the cockles of my heart.

Adrianne's opening was an overwhelming success, which may have been due in part to press coverage from her father's murder. But, she also sold almost all her paintings. And, at the prices she commanded, it couldn't just be sympathy purchases.

Charles, Terri, and I went over together. Elizabeth Brown was already there. As promised, Adrianne introduced us to the new man in her life.

"Seems nice," I said to Elizabeth.

"I thought you two were an item?"

"Not really," I answered.

"Friends with benefits?"

"Whatever."

"You know he's going to disappoint her."

"I know. Should we say something?"

"No, it would only hurt her. Just be a friend and be there for her when it happens."

"Very intuitive."

"Avoid the cliché."

"Yes, ma'am."

Although it was a good party, I was tiring quickly. Elizabeth noticed: "Would you like me to take you home?"

"That would be nice. Yes."

Acknowledgements

Despite the fact that most writers appear to work in solitude, we are, in fact, social creatures. And, we owe heartfelt thanks to friends and family who encourage us in what seems to be a driven pursuit. To all of you have ever asked, even in the most casual way, "Are you working on anything?" or, "How's the new book coming?" My sincere thanks. It really means a lot.

As always, there are a few individuals who I would like to single out for their help with *Fat Chance*. Specifically, Kamala VanderKolk, Susan Lupo, and Cindy Livingston. Also, my wife Jan. Without her generosity of time and talent—not to mention patience with me—none of this would be possible.

The 5th Estate

Honorable mention,
Southern California Book Festival

When journalist Sebastian Wren is visited by the daughter of an old flame he works to solve the dual mysteries of her paternity and her mother's kidnapping.

Ursula's Yahrtzeit Candle

One of three finalists for the
Colorado Authors' League prestigious
Award for Best Adult Literary Fiction

Ursula Frank, an 87-year-old woman, who fled Nazi Europe meets an Hispanic youth about to join a gang and, by telling her life story, shows him a better path.

Innocent Bystander

Innocent Bystander explores the ordeal that one man faces when considered a suspect in a violent sex crime, and the resulting fallout with his wife, children, and colleagues. Is there such a thing as "innocent until proven guilty" anymore?

www.ingramcontent.com/pod-product-compliance
Lightning Source LLC
Chambersburg PA
CBHW071620030726
47598CB00001B/361